An Accidental Proposal

A Pride and Prejudice Novella

Melanie Rachel

Contents

Chapter One

E lizabeth was shocked into stillness.

He *loved* her?

Mr. Darcy stood across the room, a smug expression on his face, obviously in no doubt of her reply to his proposal. It annoyed her, but Elizabeth was too chagrined to work herself into a temper about it. What a fool she was, refusing to see what had been so obvious to others! Had not Charlotte spoken of his attentions more than once? Had not Miss de Bourgh herself invited her to tea and claimed, with evident pleasure, that Mr. Darcy was fond of Elizabeth?

She had not believed them, though her anger towards Mr. Darcy had eased a bit. But even if she had been entirely convinced he thought well of her, could she have accepted that he *loved* her? And further, if she had accepted that he loved her, could she have anticipated that he would *propose* to her?

No, *this* she could not have foreseen.

Many less than flattering words had followed Mr. Darcy's statement of admiration, after all. He had declared his intentions, then detailed the scruples he had been required to overcome to do so. Nearly without pause,

he had maligned her dearth of fortune, low station, and lack of connections, before kindly explaining that none of that mattered nearly as much
as the vulgar behaviour displayed by most members of her family.

Did he somehow believe she was unaware?

His own aunt was a self-satisfied busybody who attempted to intrude
in the lives of all around her. Yet he cared for her, did his duty by her. His
very presence at Rosings was a sign of that. Could he not comprehend that
Elizabeth could love her family while eschewing any poor behaviour on
their part?

On her walk this morning she had met Colonel Fitzwilliam, who had
cheerfully informed her that Mr. Darcy was the author of Jane's unhappi-
ness. The colonel had not known he was doing it, of course—his disclosure
had been an attempt to paint Mr. Darcy's character in the best light.

It had only given Elizabeth a headache.

She was vexed and confused. Miss de Bourgh's comment, made blithely
a few days ago, had forced Elizabeth to reevaluate Mr. Darcy's behaviour
towards her. She had almost accepted the possibility that he did not dislike
her, but the discovery that he had purposefully separated Mr. Bingley from
Jane, had actually boasted about it, had changed her mind. How could he
say he loved her and yet display such callousness with her sister?

Elizabeth glanced at her letters, hastily folded and piled on the table
nearby. Jane had tried to hide her melancholy, but Elizabeth could read it
in every line. What she had to say to Mr. Darcy would not be welcome to
him, but she would be polite. As objectionable as she found his person just
now, she had seen that he was also a dutiful nephew and caring cousin to
both the colonel and Miss de Bourgh.

No. As much as she would prefer to deny it and cling to her previous
hate—well, perhaps it had only been a strong dislike—Mr. Darcy could
not be all bad. Had not even Mr. Wickham said as much? That Mr. Darcy

could please where he liked? Elizabeth felt a little flash of pride that Mr. Darcy would choose to single her out in such a way, for apparently, he did not do so often. She would not reward Mr. Darcy's proposal with vitriol. She was a lady. She would act like one.

Darcy was delighted. After months of struggling against his inclination for Elizabeth Bennet, he had finally given in to what he had long wished for and proposed. But even as he congratulated himself for overcoming every objection to Elizabeth as an eligible match—and the objections were substantial—he somehow understood that she had yet to make her answer. His elation began to curdle as he lifted his head to look at her.

She was studying him intently, her fine eyes dark and unfathomable.

It was unnerving.

Miss Elizabeth took a breath, pushed her shoulders back, and parted her lips to speak.

But her acceptance of his suit was interrupted by a loud crash outside the room. Her head turned quickly to the door as his cousin Fitzwilliam burst inside. His hair was mussed, and he was breathing hard, as though he had been running.

Darcy silently cursed the man's timing.

"Colonel Fitzwilliam," the manservant announced helpfully from the doorway.

What was Fitzwilliam doing here? Darcy had slipped out before tea when he had learned Elizabeth had remained at the parsonage. His plan to remain undetected relied upon Fitzwilliam remaining at Rosings to distract Lady Catherine.

"Thank you, John," Miss Elizabeth said. "You may go."

They waited while Fitzwilliam caught his breath. "Darcy," he said at last, casting a furtive look at Miss Elizabeth, "let us return to Rosings. I have not seen you today, and there is something we ought to speak of."

"Too late, Colonel," Miss Bennet said.

Too late for what? Darcy lifted an eyebrow at his cousin and waited.

Fitzwilliam grimaced. "Miss Bennet was distressed when I mentioned the story you related to me on our journey here. The one about Bingley?"

Darcy had not mentioned Bingley's name when telling the story of separating a friend from an unsuitable match, but of course Fitzwilliam had correctly identified Bingley as the man in his story. It was not a tale Fitzwilliam ought to have told anyone else, but why would Miss Elizabeth be distressed? She should be pleased her sister would not be forced to marry a man she did not love. And what did that have to do with his cousin's purpose for coming here tonight?

"Moreover," Fitzwilliam said through gritted teeth, "I said you should *court* the girl, Darcy, not propose to her in less than a fortnight. For a man who is so careful, I would not have thought it necessary to explain the difference."

"You advised him to court me?" Miss Elizabeth inquired. Why did she sound so . . . *astonished*?

Fitzwilliam lifted his shoulders.

Miss Elizabeth turned to face Darcy. "And when was that supposed to occur?"

The surprise nearly choked him. Supposed to? "All those walks, our conversations at Rosings—I thought . . ."

Understanding, or something akin to it, worked its way across Miss Elizabeth's countenance while his cousin dragged one hand down his face and groaned.

"Richard!" came a female cry from the hall.

They both turned to the door. "That is Anne," Darcy said, dumbfounded. "Why is she here? *How* is she here?" Had she come on foot? He stepped into the hall to find Anne struggling to catch her breath.

The manservant motioned to Anne and opened his mouth to announce her, but Darcy waved him off.

"Oh, Darcy," Anne said, between great heaving gasps. She placed a hand on her stomach and leaned slightly forward as she fought for breath. "Where is Richard?"

Anne never left Rosings unless it was to step into the gardens. Finding her here, a half-mile from the house and in physical distress, was not something he could ignore.

"He is inside, Anne." Darcy took her hand in his own and wrapped his other arm around her waist, leading her to a soft chair in the parlour. "Here," he said gently, and helped her to sit. He crouched before her and peered up into her face. "Lean back and take slow breaths."

"Annie?" Fitzwilliam, just recovered himself, sounded bewildered. "Whatever are you doing here?"

Miss Elizabeth poured a glass of water and offered it to Anne, who took it gratefully.

"I do not wish to be impolite, sir," Miss Elizabeth said to Darcy once Anne's breaths began to slow, "but have you deprived your aunt of all her company at once? I fear she will not be best pleased."

"No, I . . ." Darcy took a breath and focused on Anne. "I had intended to come alone."

"I did not see you leave," Anne admitted a few minutes later as she sipped a little water. "But when Richard disappeared, I realised you were gone too, and understood where you must be headed. I followed immediately after Richard to stop him from interrupting." She frowned at Fitzwilliam. "You are very fast."

How would Anne surmise what he had been about? And why would she seek to stop Fitzwilliam from interfering? Darcy took the glass from Anne. "Are you feeling better?"

She straightened in the chair. "There is nothing wrong with me that more frequent exercise would not cure. I might not have to argue with Mother just to walk out in the sun every so often if you wed Miss Bennet."

Miss Elizabeth made a muted sort of sound that Darcy tried not to classify as either disgust or horror. He flushed with embarrassment. Did she truly think so ill of him?

Anne turned her attention to Miss Elizabeth. "My cousin Darcy is truly a gentleman. When I said so, you agreed, did you not? And he cares for you. I was sure I had convinced you—what else is there to know?" Her cheeks were flushed pink, and after a few more gulping breaths, she no longer displayed any symptoms of illness.

Conversations? They had spent their visits speaking of him? He had been surprised but pleased to learn that Anne had invited Miss Elizabeth for tea on more than one occasion, but he had no thoughts of being the topic of their discussion. "May I inquire why my character has required your defence, Anne?"

Anne sighed. "Because for all you are a clever man, Darcy, when it comes to women you are a dullard." She turned to Fitzwilliam. "Now, Richard," she said sternly, "what are *you* about?"

Fitzwilliam's expression was contrite. "I meant to warn Darcy not to . . ." he waved his arm in a way that encompassed the entire room. "This morning I came across Miss Bennet as I took my tour of the park, you know, as I do every year. Miss Bennet and I spoke, and I said something about Darcy that upset her."

"You upset her?" Darcy asked sharply, turning to glare at Fitzwilliam. "What precisely did you say?"

"He mentioned that you congratulated yourself on lately saving a friend from an unequal alliance," Miss Elizabeth replied. "I understand there were some strong objections to the lady?"

Darcy's heart pounded in his chest as he met her gaze. If the fire in her eyes had been real, it would have reduced him to ashes.

"I presume you were referring to my sister Jane," she said, tipping her head slightly to one side. "Tell me, Mr. Darcy, what objections could you possibly have to her? For surely *she* is more than tolerable."

Anne threw a cushion from the settee at a suddenly pale Fitzwilliam. "Idiot. I had Miss Bennet convinced to give Darcy a chance, and now you have ruined it with your loose lips."

"I was trying to help!" he protested weakly, picking up the cushion and dusting it off.

"He did not ruin anything," Darcy replied seriously, his mind racing to recall why the word "tolerable" was so familiar. "I did separate Bingley from Miss Bennet's sister, and I cannot be sorry for it."

Fitzwilliam silently handed the cushion back to Anne, and she threw it at Darcy. He grabbed it out of the air before it could hit him and placed it out of Anne's reach.

"Miss Bennet—Miss Jane Bennet—did not love Bingley," he added.

"Says the man who believes we were courting," Miss Elizabeth said tartly.

A laugh escaped Anne, who clapped a hand over her mouth at the same time that Fitzwilliam made a dry, coughing sound.

"What do you mean?" Darcy asked, disappointment and bemusement making him wary.

"Mr. Darcy," Miss Elizabeth said, exasperated, "you did not even know what *I* was thinking, and you *proposed* to me. How well could you possibly know my sister, with whom I do not believe you have once held a proper conversation?" She took a deep breath and continued, rather too calmly, "Your judgment in this area is not as sound as you might like to believe."

It was as though someone had struck him. "Do you mean to tell me your sister *did* have feelings for Bingley?" He had watched Miss Bennet closely at Bingley's ball, and he had not detected anything of the sort.

"*Has* feelings, sir," Miss Elizabeth responded plainly. "She loved him last autumn, and though it is my opinion that he does not deserve her, she loves him still."

Bingley did not deserve Miss Jane Bennet, a woman with no portion and a wild, ungovernable family? Was the woman mad? Darcy's protest died in his throat when he recalled how miserable Bingley had been all winter. Had Miss Jane Bennet been unhappy too? Was it possible that the eldest Bennet daughter had wished for Bingley's addresses?

A sense of gloom settled over him. He had separated Miss Elizabeth's dearest sister from the man she loved. He had believed he was doing right by Bingley, but what if he was wrong? Miss Elizabeth certainly had better knowledge of her sister's sentiments than he. If she was correct, and she very likely was, he was responsible for Bingley's misery as well as Miss Bennet's.

Had he destroyed his own chances with Miss Elizabeth by stepping between the two? Bingley had sought his advice, and Darcy had only been attempting to help.

"It is not only that, Darcy," Anne instructed him, "you must apologise to Miss Bennet. Clearly you find her more than tolerable. Why you ever said such a thing only proves you require supervision whilst in company."

It came back to him then. The assembly. Dear God, he had said . . . "I must offer my most abject apologies, Miss Bennet. There is no excuse for my churlish behaviour."

"There is not," Miss Elizabeth replied, though with less heat than before. "Only imagine your own response had such a comment been made about a young woman in your family."

"I would be incensed," Darcy said quietly. And he would have been. No one would dare say such a thing about Georgiana or even Anne. Not in their hearing, at least. Certainly not in his. But Miss Elizabeth had no one to stand for her. Her father had not even been in attendance.

There was only one idiot in the room, and it was not Fitzwilliam.

"Very well," Miss Elizabeth said, waving one hand as though to wash it all away, "you are forgiven. But this matter with my sister cannot be so easily dispensed with."

"Darcy," Anne said imperiously, "you will write to Mr. Bingley and tell him Miss Jane Bennet cares for him."

Despite the fact that Anne sounded entirely too much like her mother, the idea was sound. Yes. It might work. He would do it right away.

Before he allowed himself to be carried away by actions that suited his own aims, however, he recalled that it had been some months. Perhaps it would be best to . . . He glanced at Miss Elizabeth. "I will of course write a letter, if that is what *you* would wish, Miss Bennet."

"I do not know anymore." Her little chin quavered slightly, and Darcy was further mortified. Whatever distress she was experiencing was his fault, and the pain of his remorse was intense. "If Mr. Bingley no longer holds the same sort of affection for my sister, then no. I would not have him visit her only to offer false hope."

"I cannot know his feelings now," Darcy said quietly. The last time he had met Bingley, his friend had appeared to be pining, but they had not spoken of it. According to Miss Elizabeth his judgment in such matters was suspect, and he began to believe she was correct, particularly regarding her sister.

"Simply warn him that he should only contact Miss Bennet's sister if he is serious about pursuing her," Fitzwilliam advised. "Will that do, madam?"

Miss Elizabeth thought carefully before replying. "Yes. That would do." She addressed Darcy. "I can write out the direction for you, if you believe your friend would like to visit Gracechurch Street."

"That was clever, Richard," Anne murmured loud enough to be heard by all.

Gracechurch Street. Darcy allowed the name of the street to pass without comment. "Very well." He was still uncomfortable with the impropriety and the low connections of the Bennet family, but had he not pushed those concerns aside in his own case? To have Miss Elizabeth as a wife would be worth suffering the company of a few ill-behaved relations, even those active in trade, and if Bingley felt the same . . . Darcy put up with Lady Catherine every year, after all. He would be a hypocrite to deny Bingley the opportunity to make amends to Miss Jane Bennet if there was true affection between them. If he found it necessary, Bingley could limit their exposure to the less proper members of the Bennet household simply by not renewing the lease on Netherfield.

"Thank you," Miss Elizabeth said.

"You need not thank me for correcting an error," Darcy assured her. He was embarrassed to have been so badly mistaken, and it was his duty as a gentleman to make amends. It was a risk to press forward before he had actually done so, but if he did not inquire now, he might not be offered another chance. "Miss Elizabeth, would you do me the honour of another audience once that task is complete? I have obviously made a hash of this, but I would appreciate the opportunity to speak with you about what I said earlier."

Anne rose from the settee, took a few mincing steps to reach him, and lifted herself on her tiptoes to whisper in his ear, "Well done." But there was only one woman whose approval he sought.

Miss Elizabeth's cheeks pinked. She looked at Anne, who nodded eagerly, but then considered him seriously for some seconds before replying.

"Very well," she said at last, and Darcy exhaled sharply in relief. "Once you have sent your letter, you may call. But be forewarned, Mr. Darcy. There is more we must discuss."

Chapter Two

T he hush that fell over the parlour after Elizabeth's acquiescence was shattered by Mr. Collins's shout from the entry hall. "Cousin Elizabeth!"

Mr. Darcy startled and whipped about towards the sound. In so doing, he collided with Miss de Bourgh, who still stood very near him. She toppled backwards, her arms waving in the air. Mr. Darcy's large hands wrapped themselves around her upper arms and prevented her from falling before murmuring something to Miss de Bourgh, possibly inquiring whether she was well.

Elizabeth was surprised to find herself piqued at their intimate pose.

The knob on the door turned.

Colonel Fitzwilliam moved so quickly and separated the pair with such sudden force that Elizabeth hardly saw him move until Mr. Darcy was sent reeling in her direction, trying unsuccessfully to remain upright, and Miss de Bourgh was again sent tripping backwards.

Colonel Fitzwilliam, now occupying the place where Mr. Darcy had been standing, wrapped one arm around Miss de Bourgh's waist and bent forward, holding her suspended mid-fall. Mr Darcy was unable to remain standing and landed heavily on one hand and a knee, just at Elizabeth's feet.

It was all such a flurry that Elizabeth was not sure where to look first—at the colonel and Miss de Bourgh, whose eyes were locked upon one another's, or Mr. Darcy, who was currently gazing up at her from the floor.

Charlotte peeked around the door. "Eliza?"

Elizabeth's hostess froze in the doorway, her gaze moving quickly from one person to the next. Then, in the calm, even tones that she had employed with Elizabeth more than once, she said, "I did not expect to find you downstairs." She pulled the door nearly closed and spoke to someone behind her. "Good night, Maria."

Mr. Darcy used the reprieve to hurriedly stand, straighten his waistcoat, and step a respectable distance away.

"I left my room for a time to read Jane's letters," Elizabeth told Charlotte when the latter turned back to them, nodding at the stack of her sister's missives. "I was not expecting visitors."

"Darcy has proposed to Miss Bennet," Miss de Bourgh announced proudly over the colonel's shoulder. Colonel Fitzwilliam finally set her upright, though he did not release her. "Is that not right, Darcy?"

Cheeks burning, Elizabeth peeked past Charlotte. Polly and John were standing in the hall, no doubt listening to every word. As Charlotte opened the door a bit wider, Elizabeth saw a few other servants in the hall too, including a man wearing Rosings livery whom Elizabeth did not know. Had the cushion been within her grasp, Elizabeth would have thrown it back at Miss de Bourgh.

"He did," Fitzwilliam confirmed grimly without sparing either of them a glance.

Mr. Darcy's expression suggested he might wish to throw something much heavier at the colonel.

"Miss Bennet is considering the offer," Miss de Bourgh continued helpfully.

Elizabeth sat heavily. Mr. Darcy looked away.

"I see," Charlotte remarked, her sharp gaze on Elizabeth. She turned her attention to the other two visitors in her home. "And you, Colonel?"

"Me?" Fitzwilliam blinked, obviously startled to be addressed.

Charlotte lifted her eyebrows and gestured minutely to his arm, still around Miss de Bourgh's waist.

The colonel made certain Miss de Bourgh was steady on her feet, then removed his arm and tugged at his cravat. "I . . ."

Whatever he was about to say was lost in the cacophony of sound and movement of Mr. Collins, who had finally realised that something of import was occurring in his home.

"Mr. Darcy, Colonel Fitzwilliam . . . Miss de Bourgh!" he cried. "Lady Catherine has sent out footmen to locate you all. She is most displeased at having been abandoned for tea, most unhappy! You must return to Rosings at once!"

"Mr. Collins," Charlotte said quietly, glancing behind her at the staff, "let us not be too hasty. I believe we are interrupting a proposal of marriage."

"A proposal?" asked her husband, waiting for the notion to catch up to him. "Oh!" he exclaimed, clapping his hands together in delight. "Mr. Darcy has proposed at last, and in our own humble abode! Her Ladyship will certainly forgive all when she learns of this! I am sure she will desire that the banns be called as soon as . . ."

"No!" Mr. Darcy nearly shouted at the same time as both his cousins, breaking into what threatened to be a very long speech by Mr. Collins. They all looked at one another, collectively abashed at their lack of manners, and Elizabeth had a sudden vision of them all as misbehaving children.

"Then what is happening here?" Charlotte inquired evenly. "Eliza, perhaps you might enlighten us?"

Elizabeth glanced at Mr. Darcy and paused. "To be honest, Charlotte, I am not entirely sure myself."

"This is all most improper, Cousin Elizabeth," Mr. Collins said, ignoring everyone from Rosings as he narrowed his eyes at her.

"I beg your pardon?" Elizabeth replied, both affronted and more confused now than she had been even a moment ago. "What have *I* done?"

Her cousin straightened to his full height. "You have kept Lady Catherine's family from attending her."

"Mr. Collins," Mr. Darcy said, nearly growling, "Miss Bennet is not in any way responsible for our presence here."

That was not entirely true, though she had not invited them.

Her cousin drew himself up to his full height, which was only a few inches shorter than Mr. Darcy. "Why are you here, sir, if not to propose to your cousin Miss de Bourgh, when she has been waiting patiently for you to fulfil your promise?"

Mr. Collins's questionable logic flummoxed her. Why in the world would Mr. Darcy choose Hunsford cottage to propose to Miss de Bourgh, if such had been his intention? There must be a hundred private places at Rosings for such a meeting.

"There is no promise!" Miss de Bourgh cried, jolting Elizabeth from her thoughts. Despite Miss de Bourgh being the daughter of his most revered Lady Catherine, Mr. Collins either did not or would not hear her.

"My cousin Elizabeth is at the root of this, for why would she claim a headache when she meant to entertain?" Mr. Collins turned to Charlotte.

"Mr. Collins," Charlotte said quietly, "Eliza would never do anything of the sort. Kindly cease insulting my guest."

Mr. Darcy took a step in Mr. Collins's direction. "You had best listen to your wife."

For a brief, tense moment, the men glared at one another, and Elizabeth feared it might come to blows. She had not thought her cousin brave enough to face down Mr. Darcy, even on behalf of his beloved Lady Catherine. It seemed a strange time for him to discover his courage.

A little piece of her heart whispered that Mr. Darcy's defence of her made her feel safe despite the turmoil.

The voices of the gathered servants rose to a low hum, though she heard the colonel and Miss de Bourgh's names being whispered rather than hers and Mr. Darcy's. Elizabeth frowned and glanced over at the colonel. He was looking in the general direction of the staff—he had noticed them as well.

Mr. Darcy was glaring at Mr. Collins when Charlotte's husband said haughtily, "I must return to Rosings to inform Lady Catherine what has happened here tonight. She will undoubtedly insist that Mr Darcy conduct himself honourably and engage himself to Miss de Bourgh." He was walking from the room, calling for his hat, when the colonel spoke.

"I have asked Anne to marry *me*," he announced abruptly to the room, his manner a bit wild.

Mr. Collins spun back to face them all, but he did not respond. In fact, Colonel Fitzwilliam's declaration shocked everyone other than Charlotte, who simply turned her attention away from her husband and back to the colonel and Miss de Bourgh.

Miss de Bourgh gazed up at the colonel, and her complexion first softened and then brightened. "That is not true," Miss de Bourgh said.

The colonel's countenance flushed a deep red.

"He has not proposed yet. However," she said with a little smile, "he was about to."

Colonel Fitzwilliam blinked, glanced around the room, and then took Miss de Bourgh's hands. "Will you have me, Annie?" he asked stiffly. "You need not, if you do not like it. I am convinced you have been hoping for more than an old soldier . . ."

Miss de Bourgh huffed. "You are only thirty, Richard."

His smile was troubled. "I am yours if you want me."

Elizabeth could not imagine a less romantic proposal—and from the charming colonel, too! Even Mr. Darcy had said he ardently admired and loved her before he had been interrupted. At least he *believed* himself in love. Did not the colonel?

"Of course I will marry you, Richard," Miss de Bourgh said. "I should like to marry you very much."

Despite her brusque manner, Miss de Bourgh was a kind person, and Elizabeth was pleased to see her looking so content. But she was worried.

Had it been only a few weeks before that she had called Miss de Bourgh sickly and cross? She had nearly crowed the words to Maria, gleeful that Mr. Darcy, who had so disparaged her own beauty, was to be married to a woman with far less in the way of feminine attractions. It made Elizabeth a little ill to recall it.

Over the past week and several visits, Miss de Bourgh had asked Elizabeth a little about herself, and then spent time extolling Mr. Darcy's character. Elizabeth had thought it possible that Miss de Bourgh's vision of the man was more compassionate than he deserved, but now she wondered. When his error about Jane had been pointed out, he had agreed to write a letter to Mr. Bingley. Of course, he had not apologised for his interference, only for his flawed understanding of Jane's sentiments.

That Mr. Darcy had believed himself to be courting her was ridiculous, of course, but it was also somehow endearing. Elizabeth had thought him haughty and disdainful, but obviously he could be as uncomfortable and bumbling as anyone else. It made him more human, more approachable. More . . . likeable.

Elizabeth was conflicted. She did not like it.

"And you, Eliza? Are you considering Mr. Darcy's proposal?" Charlotte asked, startling Elizabeth back into the present. It was unlike Charlotte to be so intrusive, and Elizabeth looked over at her, confused.

Her friend just lifted her brows.

As her mind cleared, Elizabeth noted that Charlotte had not asked whether she had accepted Mr. Darcy's offer but rather if she was *considering* it. Charlotte was intervening to give Elizabeth time to think rather than being forced to make an immediate decision.

"She *cannot* consider an offer from Mr. Darcy," Mr. Collins protested, but no one paid him any attention.

Tonight, Mr. Darcy had come to Elizabeth's defence against Mr. Collins, and the tender way in which he had ministered to Miss de Bourgh—rather like a concerned older brother—showed her that he took care of those he loved. She had to allow that Miss de Bourgh's characterization of him, while perhaps somewhat prejudiced in Mr. Darcy's favour, had thus far been accurate.

"I have agreed that Mr. Darcy may call," she said at last, and was rewarded with a small but genuine smile from her suitor. How strange it was to apply that word to Mr. Darcy, of all men.

Charlotte appeared satisfied, but Mr. Collins protested vociferously. "This is not at all what her Ladyship intends. Mr. Darcy must propose to Miss de Bourgh."

"Mr. Collins," snapped the lady in question, "I should not accept a proposal from Darcy even were I not already engaged to Richard. I am of age and may choose my husband for myself. You, sir, will tend to your own business."

Elizabeth almost felt sorry for Mr. Collins. After all, Miss de Bourgh had displayed an unseemly interest in *Elizabeth's* marital choices. But as she pondered the events still unfolding before her, she concluded that the colonel and Miss de Bourgh might indeed do very well together. She could only pray that the colonel was as pleased with Miss de Bourgh's acceptance as she seemed to be with his proposal, for his expression was a good deal more difficult to read.

"Miss de Bourgh," Charlotte said softly, "I understand your frustration, but kindly recall that you *are* conducting your affairs in Mr. Collins's parlour. Your mother will be displeased with your engagement, and she is sure to place some portion of the blame upon him. He is not without his own interests in this matter."

Mr. Collins glanced at his wife. Her earlier reproof of his conduct was evidently forgotten, for his expression was pleased and proud. He straightened his shoulders and faced his visitors with a dignity Elizabeth had not seen in him before.

"That is true," Miss de Bourgh replied. Her words were not precisely repentant, but they were calmer. "I do apologise, Mrs. Collins, Mr. Collins. I suppose I must admit to some impatience in this matter. My mother has been informed many times that I would not marry my cousin Darcy. If she is disappointed, it is her own doing."

Charlotte placed a hand on her husband's arm. "You see, Mr. Collins? Lady Catherine is already aware. I suspect, in fact, that she would prefer to handle this matter within her family. We would not wish to overstep."

There was a pause, and then Mr. Collins, befuddled, agreed with his wife. "No, no, we would not wish to offer any offense." He inclined his head in his wife's direction. "Are you sure, my dear?"

"As sure as I can be, husband. Shall we see our visitors out now? The hour grows late, and Lady Catherine is searching for her daughter and nephews."

"Of course, of course. Thank you all for visiting," Mr. Collins said, waving them all out of the room, very carefully *not* looking at Elizabeth.

Miss de Bourgh glanced at her. "Will you call on me tomorrow at our usual time, Miss Bennet?"

"If you wish," Elizabeth told her.

Mr. Darcy took a few steps to stand before her as Anne returned to her betrothed. "I will write to Bingley tonight and send the letter express first thing in the morning. May I then escort you back to the parsonage at the conclusion of your visit with my cousin Anne?"

Elizabeth offered him a single nod. The events of the evening, especially everything that had happened in the past hour, felt entirely unreal.

The gentlemen bowed, Colonel Fitzwilliam offered Miss de Bourgh his arm, and Mr. Darcy trailed out the door behind them. Elizabeth watched through the window as the trio of cousins walked the path to the lane and into what Elizabeth was certain would be a terrible maelstrom.

Chapter Three

They strolled slowly back to Rosings, not only for Anne's comfort but to delay the inevitable confrontation awaiting them. Darcy dreaded it.

Anne nearly bounced with each step. "You owe us each five pounds," she said abruptly.

Darcy rubbed the back of his head. "I do not recall placing any wagers." He thought back to Easter dinner and how, after the party from the parsonage had left, his cousins teased him endlessly about Miss Elizabeth. But he had not wagered.

"Richard said Miss Bennet did not universally admire you *or* Pemberley. Tonight proves it, for you know as well as I that most ladies of the *ton* would not have allowed you to kneel before them without securing you in marriage, accident or no. We both wagered, and our forfeit has always been five pounds."

Fitzwilliam chuckled. "She has you there, Darcy."

This was absurd. He had only been on one knee because Fitzwilliam had shoved him away from Anne. He glanced at his cousins, and his ire melted away. Years had passed since they were children together, mimicking their parents' wagers at cards with toys and sweets, and many had not been good ones. "I feel I must point out that Miss Bennet has neither accepted nor declined my proposal," he replied drily. "The two of you barged in before she had the chance."

Fitzwilliam barked out a laugh. "You are welcome."

Darcy knew with certainty that he had escaped a rejection, and he was glad of it. But he would not tell Fitzwilliam as much.

Anne, on the other hand, was all encouragement. "But it will be so much better once you have sent your letter to Mr. Bingley. I am sure she likes you now that I have rescued your character."

"You were not explicit before, Anne. Why did my character require saving?"

Anne frowned at him. "Did you have to insult Miss Bennet so terribly, and in public too?"

"What are you talking about?" Fitzwilliam inquired.

"The first time they were in company together, Darcy said Miss Bennet was tolerable, but not pretty enough to tempt him, even for a dance."

Fitzwilliam winced. "I say. That was not very gentlemanly, Darcy."

Darcy groaned. She had walked with him, spoken with him here in Kent. It had not been his finest performance, but he had thought Elizabeth had forgiven him. Rather presumptuous on his part, as he had offered no apology.

"However, I have been explaining Darcy's rudeness to Miss Bennet and she does not hate you anymore. Now that she is aware you really do think well of her, you may propose the very next time you meet. Tomorrow, perhaps." Anne's expression was smug.

Fitzwilliam caught Darcy's eye and shook his head a little in warning.

He need not have bothered. Darcy would not be asking for Miss Elizabeth's hand tomorrow. Recent events aside, he was not a stupid man. The woman had been taken entirely unawares by his offer, and he had a terrible feeling, knowing what she did about his role in keeping Bingley in town, that she would not wish for a renewal of his offer. She had agreed he might call. He would not spoil things by pushing for more. Yet.

Miss Elizabeth was not distant like her elder sister—she would tell him when she was ready to hear his full proposal. Unless he had entirely ruined any chance of that.

Darcy *was* grateful to both his cousins, though he would never say as much. He had meant to demonstrate the depth of his feelings for Miss Elizabeth by enumerating all that he was willing to give up or ignore for her sake, but now he understood his error. He closed his eyes briefly against an encroaching megrim.

Fitzwilliam was silent as they walked on, and Darcy hoped the man did not now regret *his* proposal. He *had* been holding Anne rather improperly, but they were cousins and Fitzwilliam had been saving her from a fall, not unlike Darcy had done. The servants had been watching and would no doubt gossip among themselves, but he and Miss Elizabeth had been present as well. There would be no real danger to either Anne or her mother if they all simply went on with their lives.

In fact, Darcy mused, there had been no reason for Fitzwilliam to have acted at all. Although Darcy had been holding Anne, they had not been in an embrace. His hands had been on her arms, that was all. It was no matter, for he and Anne had withstood her mother's matrimonial demands for years. They would not marry now simply to dispel idle reports.

What had Fitzwilliam been about?

Rosings loomed ahead, and his thoughts turned to Lady Catherine. His aunt would be upset that they had abandoned her. She would be incensed that they had returned with Anne engaged to the wrong cousin. Not that Fitzwilliam was the wrong cousin, of course. He was the better choice for

Anne in every way, but Lady Catherine had a decided dislike of Fitzwilliam, probably because he would inherit neither a place in the peerage nor a great fortune of his own. Over the years, the colonel had learned not to speak much to his aunt, and they all muddled along as best they were able.

"Lady Catherine asks that you attend her in the blue drawing room," Baines said when they entered the vestibule.

"Mamma!" Anne called as they all entered. "You must congratulate me! I am to be married!"

Lady Catherine was reclining in another high-backed chair. "At last," she said with a sigh, her angered expression easing. "Darcy ought to have proposed ages ago. If this is what kept you away, I shall forgive you."

Anne shifted uneasily from one foot to another, and her gaze dropped to the floor. "I am not to marry *Darcy*, Mother."

"What do you mean?" Lady Catherine's eyes shot to Darcy, then to Fitzwilliam. "You are intended for Darcy, Anne. No one else will do."

"Mother," Anne said weakly, "every year Darcy travels to visit and look over the estate, and every year we tell you that we will not wed. I know you think that Darcy is the only man who will suit, but your wishes are not my own."

It was true that every year Darcy and Anne explained why they would not wed. It was also true that every year Anne would not, or could not, look her mother in the eye when she made her excuses. Darcy thought it was that as much as anything else that convinced his aunt to continue her matchmaking campaign.

"You have never spoken to me with such disrespect." Lady Catherine's eyes narrowed. "It is clearly Richard Fitzwilliam's influence." She glared at Fitzwilliam.

Darcy opened his mouth to defend Fitzwilliam, but Anne spoke first.

"No." The word was so soft he could barely hear it, but Lady Catherine did.

Her mother's reply was almost a screech. "Pardon me?"

Anne swallowed nervously. "I will not marry Darcy."

"Who are you to marry, then?" Lady Catherine inquired, though she must already know.

"Richard." It was meant to be a statement, but Anne's voice rose at the end of her betrothed's name as though she was asking a question.

Lady Catherine's gaze landed on Fitzwilliam, who inclined his head in a slight bow.

"You will not marry that man."

Darcy was growing angry now. Fitzwilliam might not be wealthy or possess more than a courtesy title, but he had always been good to both Anne and her mother, even when his kindnesses were not well received by the latter.

"Whyever not?" Anne lifted her head and stepped closer to her mother. "He is the son of an earl and as such outranks a mere gentleman."

Mere gentleman? Darcy caught Fitzwilliam's smirk and nearly rolled his eyes, but his cousin's amusement faded in the next moment.

"He is the *second* son of an earl," Lady Catherine said. "He will not inherit."

Anne pressed her lips together. "We will have Rosings."

"You are not strong enough to run the estate, and he knows nothing about the business. No, it must be Darcy."

Anne's claim was direct, but her eyes were cast down and her voice wavered. "Is that why you wish to have me marry Darcy, Mother? To run Rosings? Or did you suspect we would depart for Pemberley and leave you in charge in our absence?"

Darcy wished he could remove upstairs, but he would not leave Anne or Fitzwilliam without his support. There was also a part of him that wished to hear his aunt's answer.

Lady Catherine stared imperiously down her nose at them as though they were still small children. "Of course not. I wish to save it for *you*. But I have been mistress here for more than twenty years. Richard Fitzwilliam has never run an estate. I would not have your father's final gift to you run into ruin."

Fitzwilliam cleared his throat. "Aunt," he said gallantly, "if you will teach me, I shall prove an excellent pupil." He smiled at Anne. "I am sure Darcy would be pleased to assist us."

Leave it to Fitzwilliam to attempt charm. He must know that Aunt Catherine depended almost entirely on the steward Darcy had recommended. "Of course," Darcy said.

Lady Catherine was already shaking her head before he had finished speaking. "He is a soldier, Anne. How many months of the year will he be gone?"

Fitzwilliam took a deep breath. "It may take some time to sell my commission, that is true. However, I am aware of the responsibilities incumbent upon me once I wed Anne."

Darcy was surprised. Fitzwilliam had never spoken of leaving the army. After several mentions in the dispatches, the colonel had earned a place in London at Whitehall and seemed very happy there. Of course, neither had he expected Fitzwilliam to propose to Anne.

"Do you see, Mother?" Anne took Fitzwilliam's arm. "There is nothing to fear."

"Anne, please," Lady Catherine was nearly pleading with her daughter, something Darcy had never seen his aunt do with anyone. "You do not want this man for a husband. He is a soldier. He is too rough for you."

"I would never harm Anne!" exclaimed Fitzwilliam, affront writ clearly upon his countenance. "How dare you even suggest such a thing!"

Lady Catherine's reply was the height of aristocratic derision. "You have been to war, nephew. Do not tell me you are not a violent man."

Darcy rather thought Fitzwilliam was contemplating violence now.

"There is a difference," Fitzwilliam said flatly, "between fighting for one's country and the sort of abuse to which you refer." His expression was a mix of disbelief and pain. Despite their fractious relationship, the insult had struck him deeply.

It was time for him to step in. "Aunt," Darcy said brusquely, "you must understand that Anne and I will never marry. Fitzwilliam proposed to Anne this evening, and she accepted. Anne is of age. She does not require your permission to wed, though I am sure both of my cousins would wish for your blessing."

Darcy said all of this, yet he still wondered whether the marriage would ever take place. The proposal had been so sudden and Anne's acceptance so unexpected that he still had difficulty comprehending it.

His aunt crossed her arms over her chest. "That they shall never have."

Darcy was done. He needed some privacy to sort through everything that had happened tonight—both his cousins' engagement and Miss Elizabeth's interrupted reply to his own offer. For now, he would proceed as though Fitzwilliam and Anne would wed. "Then until and unless you relent," he said to his aunt, "we are at an impasse. Cousins, may I suggest that the three of us review Uncle de Bourgh's will tomorrow so that we may consult your solicitors?"

They both agreed to do so in the morning.

"Anne," Lady Catherine said quietly, "I beg you, do not do this."

"Good night, Mother," Anne said quietly as she took Fitzwilliam's arm and left the room.

His aunt turned to Darcy, defeat etched in every fine line of her countenance. "Nephew?"

He could not in good conscience take her side in this. "Good night, Aunt."

It was a new morning, but his aunt had not awakened with a new outlook. Lady Catherine simply stared at Darcy across the large oak desk in the study, her watery blue eyes cold and hard. "No."

"Aunt," Darcy said, repressing a sigh, "The earl is Anne's trustee, and I am authorized by him to retrieve any documents I require to act on her behalf."

"If you wish to act on her behalf, you will not allow her to wed that man."

Her face was impassive, but she was wringing her hands. Darcy softened his tone. "Help me to understand why Anne marrying Fitzwilliam is so abhorrent to you."

His aunt followed his eyes to where he was watching her fidget and crossed her arms over her chest. "There is no point canvassing the subject. I know how you will respond."

"Then there is nothing to be done." He held out his hand, but his aunt made no move to hand him the key to the safe. Darcy shook his head. "Very well." He strode to the door and opened it. "Baines, please have Houseman find a man to drill the safe."

"You will ignore that order, Baines," Lady Catherine commanded.

The butler looked at Darcy and then at his mistress.

"I will not have gossip about Rosings bandied about the neighbourhood," she said, tossing a key onto the surface of her desk. "But I will never forgive you for this." Her lower lip trembled though she took pains to hide it, and Darcy stepped forward.

"Thank you, Baines. You may return to your work."

The butler, appearing both confused and relieved, bowed and left them to their conversation.

Darcy waited for the door to close behind Baines before saying, "Aunt, please tell me why you are behaving in this way. Perhaps I can help."

She turned away to face the window. "You can have no idea how terrifying marriage can be for a woman, Darcy. Why should you? You are a man."

"Anne does not appear to be terrified."

"That is because she does not understand. Everything a woman owns becomes her husband's. Everything is controlled by her husband, even her own body. The choice of a husband is a very serious matter."

Darcy rubbed the back of his head, and his aunt turned back in time to catch him at it. He dropped his hand, embarrassed. "That is why there are marriage contracts, to protect the woman."

"And if a man decides to ignore that contract once they are wed? A woman cannot take her husband to court, for she has no standing. What recourse does a woman have that allows her to retain her independence *and* her reputation? None."

"The man's own honour would prevent it."

"And the woman must rely on him *having* honour in his every dealing with her. It is a precarious way to live, and I have seen enough to know that most men do not behave honourably with their wives."

Darcy would protest, but it was true that many men did not treat their wives well. "Uncle de Bourgh was not such a man. Can you not explain to me why you are so against Fitzwilliam?"

"Lewis was a rare exception. If he were here . . ." She shook her head. "My reasons are my own, Darcy. Men never listen to my complaints, so why bother to make them?"

Darcy lifted his brows as he watched her depart. Lady Catherine de Bourgh had a complaint for every hour in the day. His aunt was meddling and intrusive, not unlike most of her family. Sheepishly, he considered that he had acted much the same in separating Bingley and Miss Bennet.

But this was different, somehow. He had never seen his garrulous aunt so genuinely distraught.

Half an hour later, Darcy knocked sharply on Fitzwilliam's door. When Fitzwilliam's batman swung the door open to allow him inside, he found his cousin tugging aimlessly on one sleeve of his coat.

"You will need to change," Darcy informed him.

Fitzwilliam glanced down at his clothes. "Why?"

"Soon you will be the master of this estate." He waited for Fitzwilliam to deny it. When his cousin said nothing, Darcy continued. "We need to ride its boundaries and discuss a number of issues. I thought we would ride to the northern pasture, which will require a new fence before long."

"Fence?"

"We ought to begin with something simple. Houseman will ride with us."

"The steward?"

"Indeed. The man is worth his weight in gold. Treat him well, but do not rely on him entirely. Even the best of men is tempted to cut corners if he believes his employer is not attentive."

"It is the same in the army, cousin."

Darcy nodded. "The difference is that a landowner has fewer options for discipline. You must cultivate the relationship, not merely give orders. No man wants to feel unappreciated, particularly when his work is helping to line your pockets. You do not want to offend Houseman. Honest, intelligent stewards are terribly difficult to find."

"I was going to speak to Anne."

"About?"

The two men stared at one another.

"Roberts," Fitzwilliam said decisively, "gather my riding clothes. I will call you when I am ready to change."

When the smaller man nodded and removed to the dressing room, Fitzwilliam addressed Darcy. "It is not your business, of course, but then, this family does not seem to believe in privacy."

Darcy grunted. "Interesting you should mention privacy when you are the one who informed Miss Bennet that I . . ."

"Fine." Fitzwilliam raised his hand, and Darcy paused. "I wish to speak to Anne about the manner of my proposal. I worry she accepted because she felt pressured by the somewhat . . . public nature of my declaration."

"She did not appear at all dismayed, cousin. As I recall, she prompted you to speak." No, Anne seemed very pleased. Fitzwilliam, on the other hand . . .

"Even so."

"You have laid abed too long this morning. She has breakfasted already and is awaiting Miss Bennet's visit."

Fitzwilliam's brows pinched together. "I did not sleep well . . . I thought we were to go over the will?"

"I have secured a copy for us to review when we return. Are you intending to cry off, Fitz?"

"Of course not."

"I must say," Darcy mused, "Lady Catherine was none too pleased with me for opening the safe to retrieve Uncle de Bourgh's will." Darcy hesitated. "I know that you two have long been on uneasy terms, but is there something more to it? She seems truly convinced that you are not good for Anne."

Fitzwilliam shrugged. "I cannot say she is wrong. What do I know about being a husband or the master of an estate? But if you mean some *particular* sin she holds against me, well, that I do not know."

"Nothing at all? No arguments?"

"Nothing that would make her respond to me as she does. You know as well as I that she has been this way since we were young."

"Very well." Darcy took a seat and leaned back. "My first concern was why you separated me from Anne in such a way. Was it simply to extract us from what you saw as a potential compromise?"

"I acted for that reason, but to tell the truth, I am not sure why I proposed." Fitzwilliam closed his eyes and sighed. "It seemed the right thing to do, for both of you."

"And now?"

"And now I face marrying a woman who cannot really want me. Darcy, I bring nothing of note to this marriage, and Anne is an heiress. She thinks of me only to escape you."

Darcy smirked. "Thank you for that."

Fitzwilliam ran a hand through his hair. "You know what I mean."

He did. Darcy shook his head. He had offered his cousin an allowance many times. He had even offered him a small estate that had come to Darcy through a great-aunt on his father's side. Fitzwilliam had refused. "You have status as the son of an earl that Anne does not possess."

"My status," Fitzwilliam said sullenly. "Worse than useless."

"I beg your pardon?"

"I am an earl's son. Brought up to expect all the luxuries and privileges that attend that position. And yet, because I was not the *first* son, I may expect next to nothing." He turned away. "And that is what I have to offer

Anne. No worldly possessions to speak of, no settlement, no home in London."

Darcy had never heard his cousin sound so bitter. "Fitzwilliam," he said, "all I can say is that Anne has been raised by a Fitzwilliam woman. She would not accept a proposal that was in any way irksome to her. You know that she has long been adamant that she and I would not suit, despite her unfortunate desire to always please her mother. If she has agreed to wed you, particularly in opposition to Aunt Catherine, it is because that is what she wants." He wished to inquire whether it was what *Fitzwilliam* desired, but that might be a step too far for his cousin this morning. Instead, he tried to ease the tension in his cousin's bearing. "Besides, I do not believe Anne's frankness is well suited for London."

"Perhaps she pities me," Fitzwilliam said, ignoring Darcy's jest and struggling to strip off his coat. "Roberts!"

His batman reappeared with riding clothes and boots in his hands.

Fitzwilliam always required a bit of time to mull over Darcy's advice. Darcy gestured over his shoulder. "I will wait for you downstairs. Do not take too long. I must return in time to escort Miss Bennet back to the parsonage at the end of her visit."

His cousin smiled mischievously at that. "Will you soon be making a proposal of your own?"

"That," Darcy said with a sigh, "remains to be seen."

Chapter Four

"Charlotte," Elizabeth called softly as she prepared to leave the house.

Charlotte emerged from the breakfast room. "Are you off to Rosings, Eliza? Maria may walk with me this morning, and I will have Polly walk with you."

"I am sorry I have created such disruption in your household, Charlotte. It was never my intention."

"Elizabeth," Charlotte only used her full name when she was chiding her. "I am thrilled that you are taking the time to know Miss de Bourgh better. She is a lovely woman, if a bit direct. And she will soon be a part of your family, you know."

A *bit* direct? Elizabeth smiled. Anne de Bourgh was an odd woman, but a well-meaning one. "We shall see."

"*Elizabeth*," Charlotte repeated warningly. "Mr. Darcy was quite valiant in his defence of you last night. He must be very much in love, I think."

Mr. Darcy had indeed defended her, and more to the point, he and Miss de Bourgh had vanquished the worst grievance she held against him; Elizabeth did not have much left to resent there. Even his initial insult might be forgotten after Mr. Darcy's claim that he loved and admired her. Having met Miss de Bourgh and her mother, Elizabeth could see that he came by such brusqueness honestly. She wondered, briefly, what his parents had been like.

However, Elizabeth still had some doubt that Mr. Darcy's notion of admiration and love was the same as hers. His first statement last night had been that he had struggled against his feelings. If his first impulse was to deny what he felt, could he really love her enough for a successful marriage? Added to that, he seemed a man used to arranging things just as he pleased. Until she could be sure he would not extend his need for control to her, she could make no decisions. And of course, there was still the matter of Mr. Wickham.

It was enough to cause her another headache.

Mr. Darcy's behaviour had been inconsistent to say the least, but among the insults and presumptions she had also seen glimmers of a man she might like very much. Was it wrong to wish to spend more time in his company before he proposed again? Assuming, of course, that he would. After last night he might very well have had second thoughts. "I am not so obstinate that I will deny Mr. Darcy the right to make his addresses should he choose to do so," she told Charlotte. "But I cannot promise to accept them, either. I need to know him better."

Charlotte's smile disappeared, but she recovered quickly. "I suppose that is an improvement over last autumn. Only . . . do keep your heart open to him, my dear. His is certainly the best offer you will ever receive."

"Do you think there are no other rich men who would propose to me?" Elizabeth teased, attempting to distract her friend with levity.

But Charlotte was not deterred. "I do not think there are many men who would truly *love* you. Not as you deserve. Is that not what you wish for most of all?"

Elizabeth worried her bottom lip.

"Stop that," Charlotte told her lightly, but then grew serious. "Eliza, forgive me, but the only inducement Mr. Darcy has to make you an offer is your person—your beauty, your intelligence, your wit, and your kindness." She hesitated, then met Elizabeth's gaze and held it. "Apparently, he values you for yourself, far above the more material wealth or social position his marriage could easily provide for him. Consider that, if you please, among your other ruminations."

As usual, Charlotte was correct. Such sentiments as Mr. Darcy had expressed, however poorly he had done so, were rather rare. Perhaps he really did love her, in his own way. But did she love Mr. Darcy?

No.

But Elizabeth found that she did not truly think ill of Mr. Darcy. That much was certainly possible after last night. It was astonishing to her that her feelings could change so completely with a fond cousin's praises and a simple promise to write a letter. There was still the matter of Mr. Wickham's treatment at Mr. Darcy's hands, but she began to question her loyalties there. Perhaps she had not disliked Mr. Darcy as much as she believed. Yes, she could like him. She *did* like him.

What she needed to determine was whether she could love him.

Mr. Darcy was intelligent—no, he was more than intelligent, he was clever—something Elizabeth admired in her own father. But unlike Papa, Mr. Darcy was not indolent. Even when she had resented him for insulting her, she had respected his active engagement in his affairs. He travelled to help Mr. Bingley accustom himself to the life of a gentleman, so he was generous to his friends. Miss Bingley had said he wrote regularly to his sister, for whom he stood as guardian, so he was likely a good brother. During Elizabeth's brief stay at Netherfield, Mr. Darcy had also written several letters of business, both to his steward and his attorney in London. One thing she could say in Mr. Darcy's favour—he was rarely idle.

That appealed to her a great deal.

Finally, having Mr. Darcy stand up to Mr. Collins on her behalf had made her feel cherished, in a way she never had before. Papa would have counselled her to laugh at the ridiculousness of the situation, but Mr. Darcy had taken her honour and her feelings seriously enough to defend them.

Was this what it would feel like to be Mr. Darcy's wife? If so, she could not say she would be unhappy. But it was such a frightening proposition, marriage. At least, it was for the woman.

Charlotte mistook her silence for stubbornness, and perhaps a week ago it might have been. "We *all* of us have faults, Eliza. Even you."

Elizabeth gave her a reluctant smile. "You know me too well, Charlotte."

Charlotte took Elizabeth's hand and gave it a quick squeeze. "Eliza, my purpose in marrying was to secure a home of my own. You know that."

"Yes, I do," Elizabeth answered. "And while I was not generous with you when you chose to marry, I must say that you have made a good life for yourself here, and I am pleased to see it."

Charlotte smiled demurely. "Thank you. Now, while I do not expect to leave this home for many years, it would still ease my heart to know that I was responsible, in some small way, for helping you and your family into an improved situation. Will you promise to give Mr. Darcy's offer your most earnest consideration?"

It had never occurred to Elizabeth that Charlotte would regret any part of marrying the heir to Longbourn. It was not as though any of the Bennet girls had wanted Mr. Collins for their husband—even Mary had been put off when he rudely and erroneously corrected her understanding of

Fordyce—and Charlotte had waited until Elizabeth rejected Mr. Collins's offer before attempting to elicit an offer of her own.

Elizabeth could have simply released Charlotte from any sense of obligation to the Bennets. Instead, she heard herself say, "Very well, Charlotte. If Mr. Darcy ever deigns to revisit his proposal, I promise to listen."

Elizabeth was shown into the yellow sitting room as she had been for the past week and was greeted by Miss de Bourgh.

"Allow me to wish you every happiness," Elizabeth said after pleasantries had been exchanged. "I did not have an opportunity to congratulate you last night."

"No, I suppose not," Miss de Bourgh replied, a little subdued, "but I thank you. I was hoping that you might be willing to assist me with plans for the wedding breakfast."

"The person you need is my mother," Elizabeth said with a little smile, "for she has been planning any number of such celebrations for years."

Miss de Bourgh wrinkled her nose, puzzled. "But I thought none of your sisters had married yet."

"We have not," Elizabeth replied airily. "But Mamma does love to dream about it."

Miss de Bourgh giggled, and Elizabeth was startled to hear such a girlish sound coming from a woman who must be nearer Charlotte's age than her own.

"Now that we have shared the strange experience of Richard's accidental proposal last night," Miss de Bourgh said when she had recovered her more typical placid directness, "I would like you to call me Anne, if you would."

Elizabeth was surprised that such an intimacy had been offered, but she was not opposed to it. "Of course, Anne. And you may call me Elizabeth. But if I may ask—what do you mean by 'accidental'?"

"I believe Richard's proposal came as a shock even to him. I cannot be certain, of course, but I believe he separated Darcy and I because he had some misguided notion of saving the two of us from a marriage to one another. He was just too forceful when he shoved us apart." Anne's gaze was pleasantly distracted before she drew in a breath and released it slowly. "Then of course the Collinses saw, and the servants were already chattering away."

"But still you accepted it?"

"I did," Anne said, "I have been in love with him since I visited Pemberley at sixteen and he saved me, Elizabeth. I did not expect Richard to actually propose, but once he had, I could not answer him in any other way."

Elizabeth was wild with curiosity about what had occurred at Pemberley when Anne was sixteen, but she had herself under better regulation now and would not pry. "Do you know whether the colonel returns your feelings?" Elizabeth flinched when the words came out. That had not been much better than inquiring about the incident at Pemberley. She had been affected by Anne's directness and must be more careful.

Anne frowned. "Richard knows that neither Darcy nor I would have allowed the servants' gossip to force us together, not even if my mother heard about it. He had no other reason to part us. He must love me, I think."

"I do not know you or the colonel well enough to say." Elizabeth cautiously ventured a question of her own. "Anne, may I ask why are you so set against marrying Mr. Darcy? Is there something about him that you cannot like?"

Anne's expression transformed from pensive to pleased. "Darcy is steady, responsible, and honourable. Handsome too. But that does not mean I love him. We both require more levity in our lives and would be unlikely to provide it for one another. Duty can be an onerous thing without someone to share it with." She paused, looking Elizabeth straight in the eye for a moment before dropping her gaze. "And I have always wanted to share it with Richard."

Elizabeth's new friend was petite in every way, and her mischievous smile made her appear almost elfin in appearance. "Elizabeth," Anne said, "may I now take the liberties only a friend may hazard, and inquire into your thoughts about Darcy? I know you have previously considered him rude and arrogant, and I cannot deny that he does himself no favours in female company. But you must know him a little better by now."

Elizabeth sighed. "What I think is that I must now *rethink* all of my meetings with the man. You have given me a great deal of work to do."

Anne leaned back, satisfied.

"And in the same spirit . . ." Elizabeth hesitated and allowed the sentence to go unfinished.

"You wish to know what service Richard rendered me that made me fall in love with him?"

Her cheeks warmed, but Elizabeth nodded.

"You need not be ashamed to ask," Anne told her seriously. "For it was I who mentioned it and then did not explain." She poured two cups of tea and handed one to Elizabeth before taking a sip from her own.

"Darcy's father had a steward named Mr. Wickham."

Elizabeth startled and her cup rattled in its saucer. She steadied it before asking, "Mr. Wickham?"

Anne cocked her head to one side. "Yes. A very good steward, from what I am told. Unfortunately, he had a son who was nothing like him. A Mr. George Wickham."

"I know him," Elizabeth nearly whispered.

Miss de Bourgh's lips curled up as though she had tasted something sour. "How in the world do you know Mr. Wickham?"

"He is a lieutenant in the militia. His regiment spent the winter near my home in Hertfordshire."

"The militia." Miss de Bourgh set her teacup in its saucer. "Did he say he knew the Darcys?"

"Yes, he was very explicit about his expectations being thwarted."

"Well, at the very least I will insist that you discount anything he has said about Darcy. George Wickham cannot be trusted."

Elizabeth spoke in his defence despite her growing doubts. "Forgive me, Miss de Bourgh, but Mr. Wickham is greatly esteemed in Meryton."

"Yes, I am certain that he is. He has a gift for charm and glibness that neither I nor Darcy possess."

Mr. Darcy had said something similar, had he not? When they were dancing together at Netherfield last autumn, he had told her that Mr. Wickham made friends far easier than he kept them.

Anne cast her gaze down to the floor for a moment before looking up. "I can see that you doubt me, but the beast I spoke of earlier was none other than your Mr. Wickham."

Elizabeth's eyes widened in surprise. "I cannot believe it." Nor could she believe that Anne was so open about the matter.

"It is true. Mother and I were visiting Pemberley the summer after I turned sixteen, and Mr. Wickham was always about. He was pleasant and gentlemanly. Attentive. I was sheltered and inexperienced. I did not realise he was scheming to separate me from my companion." She paused. "His object was, of course, Rosings. Even then it was well known that I would one day inherit."

Unfortunately for Elizabeth's sense of comfort, she recalled with perfect clarity how Mr. Wickham's behaviour had changed towards Mary King nearly the instant the town had learned of the girl's inheritance. He had moved from indifferent to highly attentive at the news that Miss King now had ten thousand pounds. Elizabeth had excused his actions, for the lieutenant needed a wife with some fortune, but in consequence, he *had* fallen somewhat in her esteem.

"Whatever happened?" Elizabeth inquired uncertainly.

"He held me against a tree and tried to kiss me."

Elizabeth's heart stilled. She would never have thought Mr. Wickham as bad as that.

"I slapped him, but he only laughed and then . . ." Anne's complexion reddened. "He tried to carry me off. I expect he had a carriage at the ready, but where he thought to take me, I cannot say. Scotland is still a three-day ride from Pemberley." Anne closed her eyes and shuddered. "Fortunately, my cousins were nearby and heard my cries. Their presence was fortunate indeed, for we were too far from the house for anyone there to hear me."

Anne paused. She was composed as she related the events, and Elizabeth reminded herself that this incident was a decade in the past.

"Richard was there first," she said when she resumed speaking. "He struck Mr. Wickham and knocked him down. Then Darcy dragged that"—she shuddered—"*man* off to his father's study. I do not know what was said, but in the end, my uncle did nothing about it."

Elizabeth's indignation rose, but her words were measured. "I cannot fathom how disappointing that must have been."

"George Wickham knows how to spin a tale, Elizabeth," Anne said without a hint of sentimentality. "I am sure he had my uncle convinced that I was at fault somehow." She sighed. "He was rather talented at it."

Elizabeth thought of her own Uncle Gardiner, who would have dealt very differently with such a man. She flushed when she recalled that Mr. Wickham had spun just such a tale for her in regards to Mr. Darcy. Had any of it been true?

Anne was still speaking. "I was soon back in Kent, so I was never in Mr. Wickham's company again, thank goodness. Poor Darcy still had to travel to Cambridge with the lout. His father insisted they share chambers, but Darcy refused on principle. I believe for a time he even paid for his own lodgings while Uncle George paid only for Mr. Wickham's. But Mother put an end to that. She did not like how it looked for the family. She worried people would make assumptions about Mr. Wickham's parentage."

The risk for that sort of gossip had not occurred to Elizabeth, but Lady Catherine had not been wrong. People did love to assign scandalous reasons to situations they did not understand. Mr. Darcy must have been grateful for his aunt's interference. "I confess I am amazed she did not protest his sponsorship by Mr. Darcy's father altogether. What did Lady Catherine do when you told her that Mr. Wickham had imposed upon you?"

"I had no desire to see her hanged for murder, Elizabeth," Anne said wryly, "nor did I desire to leave Georgiana and Darcy orphans, for I do not believe George Wickham would have been her only victim. Richard understood, but Darcy tried to persuade me . . ."

"Persuade you to . . ."

"Darcy wished to inform my mother, but it was my decision, and in the end, we simply did not tell her."

Mr. Darcy had disagreed but had acceded to Miss de Bourgh's wishes, even knowing that because of it he would be required to suffer Mr. Wickham's company at university. He had refused to share lodgings with Mr. Wickham because he knew the sort of man his father's godson was, and still he had not revealed Anne's secret.

Elizabeth was not certain it had been the best course, but Mr. Darcy's discretion demonstrated a surprising sensitivity to Anne's wishes. It was the very opposite of what Elizabeth would have expected of him.

"Well," Elizabeth said firmly, deeply embarrassed for ever having defended Mr. Wickham's character to anyone, but most of all to Mr. Darcy, "I am honoured that you told me." She hesitated. "My younger sisters are still enamoured of the officers, Mr. Wickham included. May I write to my father of this?"

Miss de Bourgh studied her for a moment before nodding. "You may."

Chapter Five

Fitzwilliam shook his head as they discussed the boundary of Rosings where it abutted a smaller estate called Gissington Manor. "Even a fence is not just a fence."

"It never is," Darcy agreed. "Do the Botterills still own the land, Houseman? They were considering selling last year."

Houseman, a short, stout, balding man whose business mind was among the best Darcy had ever encountered, tipped his hat back on his head and wiped his brow. "They do, Mr. Darcy, and would prefer to deal with you. If you were to inform them you will remain a few days past your usual fortnight, it might make negotiations quicker."

Darcy nodded. Lady Catherine did not like to sully her hands with such business and when forced to do so made it a trial for everyone involved. Houseman had either not heard about Fitzwilliam's engagement or was waiting for an official announcement, and therefore still deferred to Darcy.

Fitzwilliam probably preferred to observe for now, anyway. He had always been able to memorize a great deal of information, which was part of why he had been so successful as a military man, and Darcy noted the intensity in his cousin's gaze that suggested he was carefully filing away names and situations.

When Houseman rode on ahead to the next broken bit of fence, Darcy moved his horse closer to Fitzwilliam's. "It is a good piece of land, and despite the recent rise in prices, I think the Botterills are willing to sell at a more reasonable rate. It is a tertiary estate for that family, and they would rather have the money. I think they will retain the house and a small park to lease out, which is just as well. You want the tenants and the farms, not more upkeep. Would you prefer to take on the negotiations, or shall I?"

Fitzwilliam thought it over. "I will observe if you do not mind."

"Of course. It will require remaining here a bit longer."

"Yes, that will be a great hardship for you."

Darcy half-laughed at that. "I do have an excellent inducement, that is true, and your own business is nearly settled." He met Fitzwilliam's eye. "True?"

"True," Fitzwilliam replied, unable to hold Darcy's gaze. "I wish you luck with your 'excellent inducement.'"

"I shall require it, I think."

"You deserve a woman like Miss Bennet, Darcy," Fitzwilliam said. "You only need to show her why. It does not require that you set yourself the labours of Hercules, just let her see the man you are. It will be enough."

"I might prefer the labours," Darcy grumbled. It would be easier to check items off a list than lay himself bare. He had been so sure Miss Elizabeth returned his admiration. It had come as a blow that she seemed to dislike him instead.

He shook his head. One thing he knew about Miss Elizabeth was that although she had a sharp tongue at times, it was most often used as a defensive weapon, to protect herself and those she loved. He just wanted to be included in their number.

Beneath her intellectual curiosity and decided opinions, Miss Elizabeth was a kind woman. She had weathered the chaos in the parsonage last evening with admirable compassion and even a little humour, when she would have been within her rights to demand they all remove themselves from her presence and never bother her again. He knew many ladies in London who would have done just that, or worse. Darcy had been kneeling at Miss Elizabeth's feet when Mrs. Collins opened the door and looked inside. Darcy had never found himself in a more vulnerable position, though had it ended in marriage, he would not have repined.

Yet Miss Elizabeth had not taken advantage. She wanted more for herself than an accidental proposal. Darcy could not express how much his already strong respect for her had grown as a result.

"The servants at the parsonage said you told Miss Bennet that you love her," Fitzwilliam teased as he guided his horse away. "If you cannot recall that, perhaps I shall have to assist you."

"I thank you, no," Darcy told him sternly. "You have already done quite enough."

When they returned to the house, all was quiet. Darcy took the final stairs a few steps ahead of Fitzwilliam, moving swiftly towards his chamber in the family wing. As he approached, he heard peals of laughter coming from the direction of Anne's sitting room. The sound hit him as though he had walked into a wall, and he stopped just as abruptly.

Darcy's father had been an excellent man in many ways, but his refusal to hear any ill of Wickham had been difficult to bear. After the double betrayal of Wickham's attack and his father's refusal to believe it, Anne had gone into a decline that had lasted for years and he had not been allowed to speak of it to anyone. But now . . . Miss Elizabeth had Anne laughing again. She could do the same for Georgiana. He was sure of it.

After a moment, he became aware that Fitzwilliam had halted beside him.

"I do not think I have heard Anne laugh like that since . . ." Fitzwilliam's whisper was painful with hope.

"Nor I," Darcy acknowledged, when it was clear Fitzwilliam would not complete the thought. "I will change and return to walk Miss Elizabeth back to the parsonage. Perhaps you should take the opportunity to speak with Anne?"

"A bath," Fitzwilliam said, still a bit dazed. "I must bathe first. I smell like horse."

"Yes," Darcy said drily. "An outstanding idea." He had ordered a bath for himself prior to leaving this morning. Fitzwilliam would have to fend for himself. Darcy had courting to do.

Elizabeth glanced up as the hall clock chimed the time. She stood and brushed out her skirts. "It is time I return to the parsonage. Charlotte may have need of me."

Anne rose as well. "I am so grateful you came to visit, Elizabeth. Do you think you might return tomorrow?"

"Of course, if you like."

"Miss Lucas may come too, if she is available. And of course, Mrs. Collins is always welcome, though her duties keep her much occupied elsewhere."

"Thank you, Anne. I shall tender the invitations." Elizabeth might have suggested Charlotte help with planning the wedding breakfast, but the Collinses had left for Kent from the church door, without any breakfast at all. That had suited Charlotte perfectly, but it meant that Elizabeth knew more about such celebrations than her friend. Indeed, Mamma's constant preoccupation with marrying off her daughters meant that every Bennet sister was intimately familiar with the requirements of such a feast. Mamma might be too interested in weddings, but in this Elizabeth agreed—such a momentous event ought to be marked with a celebration.

At least Anne was certain of her course. She was both pleased with how events had transpired at the parsonage and was determined to see them through.

Elizabeth clasped her hands together to keep them still. Mr. Darcy was supposed to walk her back to the parsonage now. If he was not here, she would know that he regretted his words last night, and she would forget that he had ever uttered them.

Her stomach was strangely unsettled.

Even if his following words had spoken of his struggles, what woman could ever forget the moment a man said he ardently admired and loved her? Regardless of whether one recalled the words with affection or disgust, forgetting them was impossible. Besides, disgust was not what she felt. Amazement, certainly. Trepidation.

But there was something very pleasing in being loved by such a man, if love was truly what he felt. Elizabeth decided that if Mr. Darcy had done what he said and sent the letter to his friend, she would wipe away what she had believed of him before and begin again.

No, that was unfair. She must wipe the past away without conditions. He had been wrong, but so had she. In the case of Mr. Wickham, she had been very wrong indeed. And of the two of them, Mr. Darcy had accepted his fault more readily than she had.

When Anne smiled at her, Elizabeth blushed. Were her thoughts so transparent? She took a little breath and moved into the hall.

Standing straight and tall, his hair carefully combed though still a touch damp, his cravat crisp and white, and his clothes perfectly pressed, Mr. Darcy met her eye and smiled.

"Miss Bennet," Mr. Darcy said, dark eyes boring into hers before he broke their gaze and offered her a crisp bow. "Good day. I trust you are well."

His smile caused her heart to thrum. "You are here," she blurted out.

Fortunately, he did not laugh at her but simply appeared confused. "I said that I would be."

Her face grew warm. Had she just suggested she did not believe he would honour his word? Elizabeth laughed, perhaps a bit too brightly. "So you did."

"May I walk back with you to the parsonage? I believe your maid is awaiting us downstairs."

"I would say 'poor Polly,' having to follow me around everywhere, but Charlotte has determined she must after the display in her parlour last night. However, Polly has a beau at Rosings and is likely only wishing I would remain longer."

"Ah," Mr. Darcy said. "I thought I saw Mabry at the parsonage last evening. I imagine that is why the Rosings staff is so well-informed about my cousins' betrothal. News travels faster among staff than it does on the mail coach."

"Oh dear," Elizabeth replied. "Do you think that will cause any trouble?"

Mr. Darcy shook his head. "It is well known that Fitzwilliam marrying Anne is not the match her mother wanted, and therefore they will hold their tongues if they wish to keep their positions. But they are still very interested."

"That is good news, I suppose."

"It is good news," he concurred. "More particularly because Fitzwilliam and Anne will be suffering all the attention while I attempt to make up for all my errors with you."

"I think the time for apologies is past," she assured him. She was startled when Mr. Darcy paled rather alarmingly.

"I understand, madam," he responded, glancing at something behind him. "You would prefer to walk back to the parsonage alone, then."

Was this what a heartbroken man sounded like? It hurt her own heart to hear it. She had experience with Jane's disappointment, of course, but her reserved sister had never . . . oh dear.

"No, Mr. Darcy." Elizabeth reached out to touch his arm as he began to turn away. "You misunderstand me."

Mr. Darcy studied her for a moment, his dark eyes assessing, before he straightened, his expression clearing. "Do you mean . . ."

"We shall begin again, if you like, only we shall be armed with the knowledge that we are neither of us as clever as we believe. I have a propensity to assume the worst, which you seem to share. Rather than judging too quickly . . ."

"We should seek confirmation from one another."

"Much confusion might be avoided in such a way." Elizabeth smiled a little.

"But then what shall we have left to debate?" Mr. Darcy responded, his own mouth curving upwards.

"Oh, Mr. Darcy." Elizabeth chuckled. "I am never at a loss when it comes to arguing with you."

The delight in Mr. Darcy's expression was lovely to see. Elizabeth found herself unexpectedly satisfied to have put it there.

"I am perfectly willing to follow your lead in this, Miss Elizabeth."

"Oh, you mean to make this *my* responsibility, do you?" Elizabeth inquired lightly as Mr. Darcy shook his head at her. "I think not. Unfortunately, we shall have to face this challenge together."

"Together," Mr. Darcy repeated softly. "Indeed."

They stood there, in the centre of the hall outside Anne's sitting room. Elizabeth found Mr. Darcy's stare much as it had ever been. But she understood it better now. She swallowed and held his gaze, her heart fluttering in her chest.

"Oh for pity's sake," Anne said abruptly from the doorway of her chambers. "Stop staring at Elizabeth—she does not like it! Simply walk her back to the parsonage, Darcy. You should be able to manage that."

Elizabeth was grateful not to have a looking glass nearby, for she was certain to be as red as an apple, and she did not wish to see it.

"Go away, Anne," Mr. Darcy scolded her, his own countenance flushed. "I do not require your help."

"I am aware. You are beyond my help. *Go.*" Anne shut the door, and Elizabeth could not help but release a laugh. A single, spluttery laugh that signalled she had no idea what she was doing, but heaven help her, she was willing to try.

"Pray forgive my cousin's brash manner. She is typically so very quiet and subdued when we visit that I will shock you now and declare that I prefer this boldness to her silence."

"Actually," Elizabeth managed to say, "I quite like your cousin. And Miss de Bourgh has been of great assistance to me in unravelling your character, sir."

"Is that so? Will you tell me of it?"

"I suppose I must," Elizabeth replied.

Mr. Darcy indicated the way forward. "Shall we?"

"I should mention," Darcy told Miss Elizabeth as they exited the house and stepped out into a gloriously sunny day, "that my letter to Bingley was sent express this morning."

"I thank you," she said quietly. "I hope it will all turn out well. Of all the Bennets, I believe Jane most deserves to be happy."

"I cannot agree," Darcy said, "but it is up to them now. As it always ought to have been." He gazed at her.

Miss Elizabeth blushed.

Darcy fisted his hands at his sides as they strolled along the path from Rosings toward the lane. He so badly wanted to take Miss Elizabeth's hand and place it on his arm, but he must be patient. She had graciously offered him a chance to put things right, and he would not ruin it by acting too precipitously.

He heard Wickham's name, which broke through the pleasant haze her previous words had created. Any mention of Wickham required Darcy's thorough attention.

He listened with a growing grimness. Anne had evidently told her of Wickham's treachery, which only reminded him again of how badly he had failed Georgiana.

"Do you believe he is still a danger, Mr. Darcy?" Miss Elizabeth inquired. "I wish to send my father a letter about Miss de Bourgh, with her permission, of course. But that incident was many years ago, and I fear my father may not take it seriously."

"Mr. Wickham *is* a danger, madam," Darcy said, his voice clipped. He clasped his hands behind his back and took several silent steps forward before pausing. "My cousin Anne is not the only woman in my family upon whom he has attempted to impose. More recently . . ."

Miss Elizabeth's eyes grew wide. "Not your sister," she whispered.

Darcy did not know how to respond. Miss Elizabeth was so clever she had worked it out before he could claim some distant relation as the victim. Not that he would lie to her. Not that he could.

"When?" she asked quietly, looking straight ahead.

Darcy clasped his hands tightly and stared at the ground as though he could open a tunnel to escape this conversation. "Last summer, about a month before the assembly."

"Is she well?"

"She is improving. Wickham convinced her that they were in love and learning that it was a lie wounded her deeply. Fortunately, he did not have the opportunity to abscond with her, for I visited early, meaning to surprise her."

"She was not in London?"

He shook his head. "Ramsgate."

"And she *meant* to . . ." Miss Elizabeth's voice dropped. "Elope?"

"She did. After he missed his chance with Anne, Wickham relied on charm rather than compulsion."

"Did not her companion . . ."

The melancholy of the entire affair descended upon Darcy, as it sometimes did. "Her companion was involved in the scheme."

"Oh no . . ." Miss Elizabeth breathed, horrified. "What a betrayal."

"Indeed."

They walked on as Miss Elizabeth absorbed that information and then asked, "How old is your sister?"

"She was then but fifteen. I suppose her age must be her excuse."

She offered him a sympathetic glance. "Fifteen is an exceedingly dangerous age for a girl. Old enough to long for romance, too young to really understand the consequences of a poor choice, all the while considering themselves quite grown-up."

Perhaps Miss Elizabeth was thinking of her own younger sisters.

"And I defended him to you the evening we danced at Netherfield! How ridiculous you must have thought me!"

He recalled that evening with perfect clarity. "I will not deny that I was angry, Miss Bennet. But my temper was directed at Wickham. I thought you deceived, nothing more."

He gave her a sidelong glance. Miss Elizabeth's brows were drawn together, and her eyes were cast down. That would not do.

"Wickham made a fool of my own father, who was a man of the world and knew Wickham far better than you. He was in other respects an excellent and intelligent man, and yet . . ."

She glanced up at him. "Anne told me as much. Which made it worse, in a way, that he did not believe her."

"Wickham assured my father it was a harmless flirtation," Darcy said, still angry and hurt after all these years that his father had believed Wickham and not his own son. "He boasted about it after, how my father would always believe him over me. Had my mother been alive she would have been livid." The pinch of pain that always accompanied speaking of his mother made him pause for a moment. "But when you were presented with Anne's story, *you* did not deny that Wickham could have acted in such a way, as my father did. Although you thought Wickham the aggrieved party, *you* still listened to reason."

She grimaced. "Not at first, at the ball last autumn. And even now with ill grace."

Darcy shook his head. "You compared what you knew of Mr. Wickham with what Anne told you, and you decided that she was telling you the truth."

"That is hardly evidence of my intellect, Mr. Darcy. No woman would relate such a story about herself were it not true. Most women would not tell the story regardless, particularly to a mere acquaintance."

"Anne was undoubtedly taking your measure from the moment you were first introduced. She is very observant, and when she saw how I admired you . . ." Darcy allowed his words to trail off.

"Then she saw what I did not."

He shrugged. "She has known me a good deal longer."

"I fear my own first impressions of Miss de Bourgh did neither of us credit." Miss Elizabeth offered him a contrite look. "But I am learning that first impressions are often incomplete ones, and I am pleased that we are becoming friends."

Did she mean him as well as Anne? Darcy offered her a small smile. "Did you not say that we would forget the past and begin anew?"

"I did say that." She arched one eyebrow. "How clever of you to ensnare me with my own words."

He chuckled. "You have caught me in my own more than once."

Miss Elizabeth offered him a playful smile. "How fortunate it is that we are no longer lingering upon old resentments."

"Or very recent ones," he said contritely.

She laughed. "Or very recent ones." Her expression transformed then, growing serious and concerned. "And . . . how is your sister?"

Darcy sighed. "She believed the villain loved her, so she was heartbroken. But she is mending."

"Good," Miss Elizabeth said, and appeared genuinely relieved. "A girl's heart can be so tender at fifteen."

"Wickham is well aware of that. I warned him not to get up to his old tricks when we crossed paths in Meryton, but that was as far as I dared go, for he has made threats to ruin both Anne and Georgie. While his offenses against Anne are so many years past that few would take notice, that is not the case with my sister."

"I see."

He frowned. "Is there aught you would have me do?"

"Might I have your permission to explain your predicament to my father?" Miss Elizabeth inquired. "He may not be the most active of men, but I hope that a threat such as this would rouse even him from his book room."

Here was a quandary indeed. Wickham was not as afraid of Darcy as he ought to be, but he would be a fool to do anything that might bring Fitzwilliam's wrath down upon him. However, the man committed foolish acts with regularity, and it was Wickham's unpredictable behaviour that had kept Darcy silent.

"I should like to confer with Fitzwilliam, as he is aware of my sister's situation as well as Anne's."

She offered him a strange look, but simply said, "Thank you."

They had almost reached the parsonage by this time, and he had not been able to address their rather unusual courtship.

Wickham ruined everything.

"Miss Elizabeth," he said formally as they reached the gate, "Would you walk with me again tomorrow? There is a great deal more to say."

She tapped her lips with a finger. "Well, I do not know, Mr. Darcy," she said mischievously. "I am terribly busy assisting your cousin with many grand plans for her wedding breakfast. She would put even my mother to shame, I am afraid, so there is a good deal of work to be done."

He smiled a little. "Then shall I walk you there and back? Perhaps we might take a tour of the park?"

"Do you have time for such an indulgence? Here I thought you so very busy and important."

"There is nothing more important to me, Miss Elizabeth." Her hand fell to her side, and her eyes met his. Darcy read interest there, but he had been wrong before.

"I will be ready at ten, sir."

"I shall see you then." He offered her a bow and watched as she strode up the gravel path and into the house.

Chapter Six

Elizabeth pinned back an errant lock of hair and checked her appearance in the glass. There. She was ready to walk with Mr. Darcy. For a moment she recalled dressing for dinner at Netherfield and dreading being in the man's company. Now she found herself anticipating it.

Part of it was curiosity, of course. This courtship was of a rather peculiar nature. There had been a great deal of discussion about family secrets and foiled elopements and not much in the way of romantic sentiments. That is, unless a few blurted confessions that were more surprising than endearing counted.

Even stranger was that Elizabeth thought she might prefer things this way. Those more traditional forms of wooing did not satisfy as well as the subjects she and Mr. Darcy had canvassed. She wanted to know him, more than she could glean in a few months of polite calls in a drawing room. Though she would not mind flowers and poetry, they were not as important to her as an honest revelation of his character.

Unlike Charlotte, who advocated knowing as little as possible about one's future husband, Elizabeth believed the opposite. Marriage was a serious business, particularly for the woman. Once her decision had been made, the course of her entire life was laid out before her. Love alone was not enough—her father had loved her mother, or so he thought on the day they had wed. But he neither admired or respected his wife, and that was not what Elizabeth wanted.

When she stepped out into the sunshine, Polly trailing behind, Mr. Darcy was just coming up the walk. "Good morning, sir," she said, and he smiled. "I began to believe you would not come."

"Forgive me, madam," he replied, "your hostess had a great many commissions for me to complete this morning."

Elizabeth lifted her brows, amused. "Did she?"

"Indeed. I was informed I had been reduced to the position of errand boy, for the colonel was not to be found."

"Does she have you fetching lace?" Elizabeth inquired pertly.

"Thankfully, no. But among my other responsibilities, I was required to deliver her menu directly to Cook. Twice, in fact, for she neglected a dish on the first that I believe to be completely out of season."

Elizabeth shook her head. "You are very good."

"To be truthful, Miss Elizabeth," he said, subdued, "Anne has never really been the same since the incident she related to you. Today she seems more like the girl I used to know."

"And by that you mean demanding?"

He chuckled. "Yes. Cheerfully so. I am grateful to see it, and if personally handing a menu to Cook is of assistance to her, I am happy to do it."

Mr. Darcy's character certainly was an intricate one. She would not have expected him to take pleasure in running up and down several flights of stairs merely to please his cousin.

She smothered a teasing smile. "Except that completing her tasks has made you late to meet me."

Mr. Darcy drew himself up to say, very formally, "Darcys are never late. I am only *almost* late, which means I am exactly on time."

"A full three minutes tardy by the parsonage clock, sir," she corrected him.

"Then I must caution you, Miss Elizabeth, for the parsonage clock is quite wrong."

She laughed a little at that. "And your evidence, Mr. Darcy?"

He produced his gold pocket watch, opened it, and held it out so that she could read the time on its mother-of-pearl face.

"Your watch is beautiful, Mr. Darcy."

"Thank you. It was my grandfather's."

"It is beautiful," she repeated, and bit her lip, "but it does not support your claim."

He made a great show of consulting it and then winding it back. He held it out to her again, entirely serious. "Now it does."

Elizabeth shook her head at him. "I never realised you were so fond of nonsense."

Mr. Darcy corrected the time and slipped the watch back into his pocket. "I am not, in general. But you seem to bring it out in me." His eyes focused on something over her shoulder. "I hope you do not mind."

"No," she assured him warmly. "Not at all."

"Well, then," he said and cleared his throat. "I believe my dainty cousin's command was that she would be busy for the next hour and that I should show you the rose garden. If you do not prefer it, I shall escort you directly to Rosings, of course. No matter what terrible punishments Anne might devise for me, I am at your service."

Elizabeth shook her head, vastly amused by his antics. "I do enjoy roses, Mr. Darcy."

There was a soft breeze as they made their way up the lane towards Rosings, and Elizabeth paused to watch the clouds being pushed across the sky.

"I believe we may yet see some rain," Mr. Darcy said.

"Bite your tongue sir," Elizabeth replied teasingly. She narrowed her eyes. "The clouds are white, and it is not at all gloomy."

He smiled. "A little rain in the spring is hardly unusual, Miss Bennet."

"But I have no umbrella, and neither, Mr. Darcy, do you," she said, glancing pointedly at his empty hands. "Therefore, it must not." She struggled not to laugh at the expression on Mr. Darcy's countenance.

"Ah," he said at last. "I see. As you apparently control the weather, Miss Bennet, I shall call on you when Pemberley's crops are in need of a bit of water."

"See that you do," she said primly. Such an expression was so rare upon her countenance that she could not hold it for long. She smiled back at Mr. Darcy and his eyes lit up.

His eyes were dark and . . . expressive. How had she never noted it before?

"This is the best time of year to see the flowers, Miss Bennet," he told her as they entered under an arch of lilacs. "Everything is beginning to bloom."

There, she thought with some satisfaction. Flowers were a more acceptable topic of conversation than elopements and family secrets. They were making progress. "Polly," she called to the maid, "we are at least within sight of the house." It was a stretch to say so, but Polly would not question her. "You may go inside."

Polly smiled broadly, dipped a quick curtsy, and hurried away.

Elizabeth looked about her. The arches were not the only place the lilacs grew. "Why lilacs?" she asked Mr. Darcy, sniffing the air and nodding at the purple blossoms. "They are an unusual choice for a formal garden."

"Anne prefers the scent."

Elizabeth recalled that there had indeed been a bouquet of lilacs in Anne's room the last time she called. "At home, they only grow along the roads and in the hedgerows." She glanced at him knowingly. "Which is where my mother believes we shall all end when Mr. Collins ultimately inherits."

"The hedgerows?" he asked vaguely.

Her eyes widened. "Forgive me, Mr. Darcy, I ought not make sport of my mother."

"No, no," he assured her. "It is well." He lifted a hand to his chest as though in pain, which she thought odd.

"Are *you* well?"

Bemused, he said, "I am. Why do you ask?"

She nodded at his hand, which he allowed to drop.

"I am perfectly sound, Miss Bennet." His brows pinched together. "Would you truly have no one who would take you in?"

It was all in his eyes, which had widened slightly. How had she ever believed them cold and unfeeling? Elizabeth could read everything there if only she took the time. Mr. Darcy felt compassion for her situation and if she were not mistaken, some alarm as well.

She hastened to reassure him. "I am pleased to say that my mother's claims are exaggerated. My uncles will see that my mother and any daughter of Longbourn who is yet unmarried has a place to live, food, clothing, everything they truly require. Mamma does dread outliving her position, of course, as do most women who face diminished consequence and income when their husbands die."

"Most certainly," Mr. Darcy replied graciously. His expression was still serious, sombre, even. "I criticised your mother without truly understanding her fears."

"Those fears are not an excuse for her behaviour," Elizabeth said gently. "But they do explain much of it."

"Indeed." Mr. Darcy straightened as they passed through to another garden. They were a good way from the great house now, though Elizabeth could easily see it in the distance. How many gardeners it must take to tend to such grounds!

The scent of the lilacs and roses were extraordinary, and Elizabeth paused to breath it all in. She could sense Mr. Darcy by her side, watching her, and, released from the feeling that he disapproved of her, his attentions made her blush. She closed her eyes, turned her face to the sky, and took another breath to enjoy this moment of nearly perfect harmony.

And then the rain came.

It happened very suddenly, as spring rains were wont to do. But this was no soft spring mist that descended upon them. It was a deluge.

Had he been at Pemberley, Darcy would have been thankful for it—rain at this time of year might be heavy but was typically brief. But he was not at Pemberley. He was with Miss Elizabeth, and he had led her too far from the house to seek shelter there in time to prevent a drenching. He had suspected it was going to rain, but Anne's directives had been the same as his wishes, and so he had ignored the weather.

He stripped off his coat, inadequate though it was, and held it out over Miss Bennet's head as they hurried in search of some shelter.

"Oh, Mr. Darcy," she said with a little laugh that warmed his heart, "I am already soaked. You ought to save your coat to keep yourself dry."

"I confess myself shocked," he told her, his solemn tone out of keeping with their behaviour, as they were nearly running to the little covered bench in Anne's lilac garden. "Do you believe I would keep myself dry at the expense of a lady?"

Miss Elizabeth pressed her lips together. "I did not mean," she began haltingly, and then hesitated. She had spotted the stone shelter. "Oh, there it is!" She hurried on and waited until they were both under cover before she evaluated him thoughtfully. "Was that a joke, Mr. Darcy?"

He smiled. "It was not a very good one if you must ask."

"It is not that, it is only . . . I am learning to understand you better, I think."

"That is good news, particularly if you at any time believed I would leave a woman standing in the rain when I could assist her," he replied, and this time, she smiled at him.

"I am ashamed to say that I might have, once. But I am very happy to have my prejudices so completely turned over."

He was at once insulted and pleased. "Miss Bennet—"

She glanced down and interrupted him with a screech.

"What is it?" he cried, half ready to do battle and half to laugh at the little jig she was dancing.

"Slugs!" she cried, shaking one booted foot away from her.

Darcy watched her cavort for a few moments, amused that a woman so stalwart as Miss Elizabeth Bennet could be undone by a few garden slugs on her boots. "If you hold still for a moment, madam, I will remove the intruders. However, we are in a garden, and it is raining. I fear there may be more."

"That is not comforting, Mr. Darcy," she said as he crouched to hold her boot steady and pluck the slugs from the leather. He swallowed nervously when he realised he was touching her little foot, but he cleared his throat, blinked, and tossed each one back into the flower beds.

"I hate slugs," she informed him with a shiver. "Nasty pests."

"These slugs eat decaying plants," he informed her. "So they are not pests."

She stared at him. "That may be so, Mr. Darcy, but I do not want them on my boots."

"So I see," he said drily. "Is there any reason you hold such a prejudice against the creatures, madam?" He straightened to his full height. "I must ask as I feel some solidarity with them where you are concerned."

She looked up at the roof of the shelter. His sister did the same at times when he had particularly vexed her.

"I am not prejudiced against you, Mr. Darcy." She paused. "Not now, at any rate. And when I was, I had cause."

That was only fair. "And the slugs . . ." he prompted, still wishing for that bit of information.

She huffed, held up her skirts a little, and turned each foot this way and that until she was sure nothing living remained on her person. "Arthur Long used to put slugs inside my shoes until I no longer felt safe to remove them at the stream near Longbourn."

"I am almost afraid to ask, but I shall. How old were you?" Darcy asked, expecting that the woman before him had waded in the stream long after society believed she ought.

"I was five, sir," Miss Bennet replied tartly. "He was ten. Horrid creatures, boys."

He laughed aloud at that. "They can be."

"I wanted to play with them because their games were far more interesting than dolls. When I was ten and Lydia was five, we had some fine sport together, for she felt the same."

"Miss Lydia was your playmate?"

"For a time." Miss Bennet's expression grew wistful. "We were great friends, once. But I grew up and I suppose . . . well, she is still very young."

"Is she?" She had to be at least eighteen, old enough to know how to behave in company.

Miss Bennet nodded. "She will be sixteen in May."

Younger than Georgiana! He had not realised—of course he had not, for fifteen was far too young to be out, even in the country, and Miss Lydia was a tall, stout young lady. Georgiana was sometimes thought older, too, for Fitzwilliam women tended toward the statuesque. Darcy, however, did not intend to allow his sister her come out until she was eighteen and he was not certain she would be ready even then. Georgiana lacked the confidence the woman before him possessed in abundance.

A thought struck him. "Miss Catherine is not your youngest sister, then?" He must pray not, for if she were, she was but a child and should never have been subjected to . . .

"Oh, heavens no." Miss Bennet grimaced. "And do not ever ask such a thing in her hearing, or Lydia's either. No, Kitty is the elder by two years."

"I would not have guessed it," he admitted. "Miss Lydia is . . ." his voice trailed off. Better not to say it.

Miss Elizabeth actually laughed a bit. "You are learning, Mr. Darcy."

He peered out from beneath the stone roof. "I believe the rain has stopped. Shall I take you back to the parsonage to change?"

"Yes, I am afraid you must. I do hope Anne is not waiting to assign you more tasks."

"There is no task more important to me than your comfort, Miss Bennet."

Miss Elizabeth met his gaze, and he nearly lost himself in the gentleness of it. How could he have believed her awaiting his proposal when she had never before looked at him in this way?

She raised her hand to her chest.

"Are you well, Miss Bennet?" Darcy inquired with concern.

"Perfectly well, sir," she said. "Shall we?"

"Elizabeth, I am so happy to see you!" Anne called when they arrived at last. She stopped to raise her eyebrows at Mr. Darcy, who took his dismissal with good grace.

"I shall meet you here after your visit," he said in a low voice, then bowed to them both and departed.

Anne rushed forward to take Elizabeth's hands. "Mrs. Abernathy, the modiste, will be here shortly. Will you help me pick out patterns and fabrics?"

"Of course, I would be pleased to do so," Elizabeth replied warily, "but should you not ask your mother to assist? If she is anything like mine, she must desire to share this moment with you."

"What moment?" Anne's nose wrinkled.

"Ordering your trousseau."

"This is not ordering my trousseau," Anne assured her. "Just a few additional dresses. I will order my trousseau in London, but until then, I want to dress more like you do."

Elizabeth pressed her lips together. Though her large personality made it easy to forget, Anne was shorter than Elizabeth and more finely wrought, diminutive but well-proportioned, like the porcelain figurines from Germany Mamma loved so much. Clothing that looked well on Elizabeth would not suit the small, slight woman before her. This was likely to be a delicate morning call.

"Do your own dresses not please you? The fabrics are very rich."

"No, they do not," Anne said almost spitefully. "They are for girls who are not yet out. Mother always said that I would order more fashionable gowns when I was married, that there was no need to put me on display since I was to marry Darcy. Well, I am to be married, and I would like gowns that please both me and my husband." She waved a hand at Elizabeth. "Like yours. Darcy is always aware of what you are wearing."

Elizabeth's cheeks warmed, and she touched her spencer uncertainly.

"Yes, precisely." Anne eyed Elizabeth's dress carefully. "Morning wear. Something nice for dinner. And some walking dresses."

Anne had become winded walking to the parsonage, but Elizabeth did not think it kind to remind her of it. Perhaps Anne meant to begin walking out more often, in which case she could only approve.

"Will you help me?" Anne's countenance was bright with hope.

Elizabeth acquiesced. "Very well. But you must promise to inform your mother I suggested we consult her. I do not wish her to scold the Collinses for inviting me."

"I will," Anne promised. "Thank you, Elizabeth."

Elizabeth sat at the table where Anne had set out all her fashion magazines. She had used bookmarks for pages with patterns she liked, and Elizabeth went through them methodically, steadily unmarking pages with dresses that she knew would not suit.

"How can you know?" Anne asked, drawing up another chair to sit beside Elizabeth. She pointed at a design with more volume in the skirt. "I think that would be pretty."

"It will be on a woman who is taller," Elizabeth said kindly. "My elder sister Jane, for example. But you and I do better with a straighter skirt."

Anne bit her bottom lip. "But how do you know?" she repeated, a bit of petulance creeping into her tone.

"Experience," Elizabeth replied with a laugh. "Between my sisters and me, we have made every mistake on a dress it is possible to make. And my mother, who means well, thinks that lace cures all." She grimaced. "In fact, my youngest sisters are still wearing gowns that are too . . ."

Anne smiled mischievously. "Too much?"

Elizabeth nodded, relieved she would not have to say so herself.

"Very well," Anne said with a crisp nod. She flipped through several more magazines, muttering to herself. "Too much. No, too much." Suddenly she stopped to pull another magazine between them and open it. She pointed at a white cambric frock with short sleeves. "What about this one? I thought it was lovely and quite suitable for the warmer weather."

"That," Elizabeth said, studying it, "is perfect. Elegant without being fussy, and if you choose the right fabric, it will not be too delicate for regular wear. I do not prefer tassels on sleeves myself, but these are small and would look charming on you."

Anne gazed down at the picture. "Then that will be the first dress I have made." She smiled widely at Elizabeth. "With the tassels. May we speak about colours, now?"

Elizabeth returned her friend's smile. "Of course. I have very decided opinions on colours."

Their eyes met for a moment before they both laughed.

Darcy made his way down to the study only to find Fitzwilliam already sitting behind the desk with piles of paper stacked haphazardly about the surface. For a moment, he was transported back to those first overwhelming days after his father's unexpected death. Several large projects he knew little about had been left unfinished, so many details kept in his father's mind, unrecorded.

"Fitzwilliam, we must speak about Georgiana."

Fitzwilliam glanced up at him blearily. "Can it not wait?"

"No. I told Miss Bennet about Ramsgate."

Fitzwilliam's gaze sharpened. "And why would you do such a thing?"

Darcy met the icy glare of his cousin. "She needs to protect her sisters."

"Our duty is to protect Georgiana."

"She has asked permission to tell her father."

"No."

"It is the right thing to do. And it is not your decision to make, in the end."

"You cannot be serious. Never mind the scandal, it would crush Georgie were anyone to find out."

"I trust Miss Bennet."

Fitzwilliam shook his head.

"What if she did not mention any names, only that she heard it from me?"

His cousin regarded him shrewdly. "You are determined, I see."

"I am."

"Stubborn as an ox, you are."

Darcy grunted. "When my cause is right, I am steadfast, that is all."

Fitzwilliam scoffed. "That is all, he says. Very well." He pointed at Darcy. "No names. And she had better say she heard it from me. Apparently no one in her neighbourhood likes you."

Darcy nodded. It was what he had intended from the start, but Fitzwilliam would have been offended not to be asked. He motioned to the mess on the desk.

"May I help?"

"Thank you, no," Fitzwilliam said, returning his attention to his work and sifting through a stack of papers. "I need to familiarize myself with the recurring expenses of the estate. One of the merchants has complained about a delinquent account." He frowned at the document and tossed it aside.

Darcy frowned. "The accounts are settled each quarter. Shall I have a look?" He stepped towards the shelf where the estate ledgers were kept.

Fitzwilliam stood. "No, Darcy. I thank you, but some things I must do for myself."

"But I could . . ." He motioned towards the ledgers. It would take him a minute or two, no more.

"*Darcy,*" Fitzwilliam said, tired and exasperated. "I will call on you if I require assistance. Will that do?"

Darcy wanted to argue that he could help Fitzwilliam avoid some of the same mistakes he had made. He had gained so much experience managing Pemberley, and although he visited Rosings but once a year, he had become quite familiar with the estate's workings. He would never attempt to school Fitzwilliam in military tactics, but this was a subject he knew very well. The rebuff stung.

"Very well," he said uneasily. "I will . . ." In truth he did not know where he would go or what he would do. Miss Elizabeth was above stairs with Anne, and Darcy had planned to work in the study until it was time to walk her back to the parsonage. He could not recall the last time he had been entirely without an occupation. Even on Sunday evenings, he read or wrote or listened to music.

It hardly mattered that he had not completed his sentence, for Fitzwilliam already had his nose back in his papers, as though Darcy was not standing ten feet away. If his cousin would only reach for the ledger. For the briefest moment, he wavered. But Fitzwilliam had summarily dismissed him. So he left.

Typically, he would call for his horse and take a ride, but that would require changing and then bathing when he returned, and he did not wish to miss his chance to walk Miss Elizabeth back to the parsonage. This morning's stroll had been delightful—he had been ridiculous, and it had felt grand when she laughed at his antics.

He informed Baines that he was to be notified when the women were finished with their visit, then wandered down the hall to select a book from his aunt's well-stocked but rarely used library. One of the chairs had been pushed near the window, where the light was good, and, propping one leg up on the ottoman, he began to read.

A few hours later, Fitzwilliam strode in. "So this is where you have been hiding yourself."

Darcy reluctantly set down his book. "I am not hiding. I was sent off."

"Do not be surly," Fitzwilliam chided. "It does not become you."

"I am only stating the facts, cousin." Darcy had quite enjoyed his leisurely morning, though he did not believe he would enjoy it as much were it not so rare an occasion.

"Not that it matters. I have solved the issue. We were indeed late, and I have sent the payment with a little extra for the man's troubles."

"You paid a merchant more than his due?" Lady Catherine burst through the already open doors of the library, and Darcy winced at the shriek of indignation. How she managed to be in the right place to overhear conversations at all times was beyond him. "If this is how you plan to run Rosings, you will bankrupt us in a year!"

Darcy grunted. If his aunt had not bankrupted Rosings with her love of china tea sets and gaudy wall hangings, Fitzwilliam was unlikely to do so. "How much?"

"You mean the extra?" Fitzwilliam was hesitant to say, now that they had company. "Two pounds on a twenty-pound account."

Ten percent. It might not seem much, but . . .

"Two pounds?" cried Lady Catherine. "Two pounds?"

Darcy stood and replaced his book on its shelf. Apparently, he would not be reading any more today.

"I thought it fair." Fitzwilliam was stout in his own defence.

Another wordless sound escaped Darcy's mouth. He could not help it.

"What?" Fitzwilliam inquired, crossing his arms over his chest and glowering at them both.

Darcy considered not answering that, but he had a suspicion and his cousin ought to know. "Which merchant?"

"Barnaby."

"Are you mad, boy? You *are* mad! Extra money for being a bit late, who ever heard of such a thing?" She pointed at Darcy. "I want you handling the accounts, Darcy. At least you know enough not to overpay!"

"Aunt . . ." Darcy said warningly.

Lady Catherine stormed out of the library, her strident exclamations audible even as she grew farther and farther away.

When the noise faded away, Darcy asked quietly, "Barnaby, did you say?"

"Yes."

"Barnaby is often late submitting his bills of sale. When did his accounting arrive?"

Fitzwilliam's eyes narrowed. "I do not know, precisely. Only that his paper was on the desk with the others, and he complained. The records supported his claim that he ought to have been paid out already."

"How late was his payment?"

"It was . . ." Fitzwilliam's forehead creased.

"Lady's Day was only a week ago. Everything that had been submitted was paid then. I saw to it myself."

"So Rosings was *not* late?"

Darcy shook his head. "Barnaby has created the pretence that he was not late at all but that the mistake was ours. His purpose was to be paid now rather than wait until next quarter for his money. He achieved that goal, and now you have paid him extra for the lie."

Fitzwilliam rubbed his temples. "How do I handle this? I do not want him to think . . ."

"No," Darcy said, holding up his hands. "If you want to learn, cousin, this is an inexpensive lesson, and one that you ought to see through yourself."

"You were eager to do the work yourself a few hours ago."

"And now I am helping by . . . not helping. You wished to learn, and I have no desire to wait upon the line of merchants who will soon be calling, looking for an overpayment of their own."

"They will not do that." Fitzwilliam let his head fall back, and he stared up at the ceiling. "Will they?"

"I am only surprised they are not lining up outside the study already," Darcy said drily. "The thoroughly honest man is a rarity. When you meet one, take note and hire him if at all possible."

Fitzwilliam sighed. "I am an excellent colonel. Perhaps Lady Catherine is right, and I should not give up my commission."

"Cousin," Darcy said with a little laugh, "this is only your first try. You will make many such blunders before you are done."

"It is a good job you did not go into the church. Your lectures are not inspiring."

Darcy smirked. "You will learn. I did. Not that I do not still err from time to time."

Fitzwilliam was silent for a minute, then sniffed. "Such as your dealings with the Miss Bennets?"

Leave it to Fitzwilliam to bring *that* up. "I meant with the estate, but very well. My errors in that quarter amount to far more than two pounds. However, *I* have not given up." It was no great virtue, for he could not accept defeat until and unless Miss Elizabeth turned him away. It had taken half a year to make up his mind to propose, but now that he had, the decision was irrevocable.

Now he had only to convince Miss Elizabeth to accept him.

His cousin leaned forward, his elbows on his knees. "It is not the same. You were brought up to run Pemberley."

Darcy sighed, recalling that time. It no longer overwhelmed him, but it never failed to bring a bit of melancholy with it. "That does not mean that I was prepared."

Fitzwilliam ran a hand through his hair in a moment of unusual distraction. "Forgive me. I know you were not expecting to inherit so early."

"It is all right." Darcy walked to the window. The sky was blue and cloudless. "You will learn from your mistakes, and hopefully I will be allowed to make amends for mine."

Chapter Seven

Sunday had passed slowly. It had rained on and off all day, and Darcy had only been able to gain a glimpse of Miss Elizabeth in church. His aunt had not lingered long enough after the service even to speak a few words to her.

Monday had dawned clear and warm. Had Anne not sent the two of them into the village to deliver a message to Mrs. Abernathy, he might have asked Miss Elizabeth to walk to the grove she preferred.

The dressmaker had departed Rosings with her instructions not an hour past, and Anne could easily have sent one of the servants. But Anne did not wish to put any of the staff in the uncomfortable position of supporting her against her mother, and so here he was.

Darcy suspected that his cousin had intentionally held back whatever information she was sending him off with, but he did not protest, for Anne had also suggested Miss Elizabeth walk with him. Normally he would chafe at such an obvious attempt at matchmaking, but for once they had the same goal.

"Glorious," Miss Elizabeth said softly from where she walked beside him.

Darcy glanced down at his companion. Though his view was somewhat obstructed by the brim of her bonnet, he could make out the soft skin of her cheek and the straight line of her jaw. Miss Elizabeth was looking about, enjoying the sunlight.

"It was just turning to spring when I arrived in Kent," she told him. "How much has changed!"

She meant only the landscape, he supposed. But he could not help thinking about how much he had changed; how his own hopes matched the season, how his heart was only awaiting her agreement to push through the soil and bloom in full colour.

"Springtime in Kent is lovely," he agreed. "It will come a few weeks later in Derbyshire."

"I have never been so far north, but my aunt lived in that county for some years in her youth."

Her aunt. The one in Meryton that was married to a solicitor, or the one whose husband was in trade? "Whereabouts?"

Miss Elizabeth's little nose scrunched up as she thought about it. "I recall her mentioning a town called Lambton? Does that sound right?"

"But Lambton is not five miles from Pemberley!" he exclaimed in surprise.

Miss Elizabeth smiled. "She told me once that she would never have left had she not met my uncle on a trip to London. Derbyshire is still her favourite of all counties."

"She is a woman of taste, then," Darcy said, hiding a smile. An aunt who appreciated Derbyshire might be an ally, should he require one. "For Derbyshire is the best of all counties. Wilder than the southern counties, not as inhospitable as those farther north."

Miss Elizabeth laughed softly. "You are determined to forgo any bias, I see."

"This is not bias. It is simply truth."

Miss Elizabeth was about to respond when they were interrupted.

"Mr. Darcy," called a gentleman approaching them.

Darcy wished the man away. "Yes?" he asked.

The young man tipped his hat and came to a stop a few feet before them. "Beg your pardon, sir. Miss," he said. "I'm Mathers, I live . . ."

"At Rosings, on the back two acres nearest the stream," Darcy replied. This must be Mathers's son, who was taking over for his father.

Mathers nodded once. "Yes, sir. I was wondering whether I might speak to you about the quality of our seed."

"Is there aught wrong with it?"

"Yes, if I may show you."

"I will send Houseman."

"Begging your pardon, sir. Mr. Houseman knows contracts, but he is not a farmer."

Neither was Fitzwilliam, but he could be a fine one if he tried. Darcy would drag his cousin out in the morning if needs must. "Very well. To-morrow early?"

"Thank you, sir."

Mathers bowed and was gone.

"What could that mean, the quality of the seed?" Miss Elizabeth asked curiously.

"Seeds do not last forever, and even those that are relatively new must be stored properly. If the seed we provided the farms is faulty, we must see to it immediately, for it will affect the harvest. It is Mr. Mathers's first season taking over entirely from his father, and he may only be anxious to do well. Of course, he is not wrong about Houseman. No man can do everything well."

"Except for you?" she asked teasingly. "Mr. Darcy, gentleman farmer?"

He laughed softly and shook his head. "I am not a student of the law, as Houseman is. No, I cannot even make such a claim in jest. The world is a vast place, Miss Elizabeth. I must be satisfied with understanding my small part of it."

She gazed up at him for a moment. Would that he could interpret her intent expression. Before he could puzzle it out, however, another man called Darcy's name and held up his hand in greeting.

Blast.

Elizabeth watched Mr. Darcy converse with others as their short walk into the village stretched past an hour. He addressed and directed five different men who had hailed him as they walked past. Tenants, shopkeepers, workers from the estate, each of them with a question they were sure could not take more than a moment to answer and always did.

Mr. Darcy betrayed no signs of irritation at the constant interruptions. In fact, he was decisive and direct. "I will look into it," was his typical conclusion, "and Mr. Houseman will speak with you."

How he kept track of it all was a mystery to her.

This proof of his acumen did not help her make up her mind about the sort of man he was, however. The men respected his cleverness, but what was he like when not speaking of business?

She soon had an answer. The final person to approach them was not a man at all, but a girl, not quite old enough to be called a woman. She dipped a respectful curtsey and then stilled, wringing her hands, as though she could not remember what she wished to say. Elizabeth was about to ask for her name, to try to make her more comfortable with an introduction, but Mr. Darcy made a proper bow and said, "Miss Addison, is it? How is your family?"

"Papa is ill, Mr. Darcy." Her voice was so low it was nearly a whisper. "The fields aren't done proper, and I can't fix it on my own."

"Where is your brother?"

"Gone off to the navy, sir." She shrugged. "He and Papa don't get on."

Mr. Darcy nodded seriously and spoke gently. "Do you have a request to make of me, Miss Addison?"

"An apothecary, sir? Mr. Morris is sorry and all, but he can't help us if we can't pay. We would have the money when the crops come in, only . . ."

Only she was not certain there would be a good crop in the autumn if her father was too ill to complete the planting now, and in a small community like this, everyone else would know too.

"Come," Mr. Darcy said firmly, and Elizabeth was not sure he was speaking only to the girl. She trailed after the pair as they entered the apothecary's shop.

Mr. Darcy called out when he entered, and the apothecary poked his head out from a back room. "Mr. Darcy, sir," he said, surprised. "Does Miss de Bourgh require anything?"

"No, my cousin is enjoying excellent health," Mr. Darcy said, and Elizabeth realized that it was true. She wondered whether Anne's health issues were truly so severe as her mother made them out to be.

"Miss Addison's father is in need of your services. Please remit your bill to Mr. Houseman."

"Yes, Mr. Darcy." The older man turned to the girl with a sympathetic nod. "Miss Addison."

Mr. Darcy turned to go, but the girl caught at his sleeve. She blushed mightily when he looked back at her, but stammered, "Thank you, sir."

Elizabeth was astonished when he patted the girl's hand and said, "Whatever can be done for your father will be, Miss Addison. You have my word."

The girl's eyes widened, and she nodded vigorously.

Mr. Darcy addressed Elizabeth. "Are you ready to continue our errand, Miss Bennet?"

"Yes, of course."

"I apologise for the interruptions. They are aware that my visit seldom lasts this long," he admitted as they finally reached Mrs. Abernathy's shop. "Many wish to have 'one more question' answered before I leave, and often that leads to several more."

"They do not wish to pose their questions to your aunt?" Miss Elizabeth inquired with a smile. "How extraordinary."

He chuckled a little at that. "Yes, well." Mr. Darcy clasped his hands behind his back as they began to walk again.

"Mr. Darcy, since you are so adept at offering answers to questions, may I ask you one?"

"Of course."

"You have met with several men today. Yet you never gave a promise to any of them. You only made one to Miss Addison. Why is that?"

Mr. Darcy's brows pinched together, making him appear very severe indeed. But Elizabeth realised, now, that it simply meant he was thinking over her words.

"I must be very careful in offering assurances, Miss Elizabeth," he said. "I never give my word unless I am entirely confident that I can keep it."

Elizabeth nodded thoughtfully. "You are entirely confident that the apothecary will be paid to tend Miss Addison's father?"

"I am."

"Why?"

"Because, Miss Elizabeth, should Lady Catherine refuse to pay, I will."

They finally reached the dressmaker's shop, and he held the door open for her. "Shall I await you outside?"

She smiled impishly at him. "More afraid of entering a women's shop than being accosted by townspeople with requests?"

He pressed his lips together and cast his eyes upward. "I should not like to leave anyone with unanswered questions."

"No, I suppose you would not." Elizabeth glanced about her. There was no one about now. "This is what I intend to send my father." She reached into her reticule and handed the letter to him. "I have not sealed it, for I thought you might wish to read it first."

He held the letter but did not look at it. "I trust you, Miss Bennet."

"Even so, Mr. Darcy," she insisted.

Darcy met her eye and held her gaze for a long moment. "I thank you."

Elizabeth nodded and entered the shop, the bells on the door ringing behind her. Mrs. Abernathy bustled out from a back room, and Elizabeth handed off Anne's note to her. The modiste opened it and frowned.

"May I assume that this was not an urgent message?" Elizabeth asked knowingly.

"Brides are often nervous," Mrs. Abernathy replied, which was all the confirmation Elizabeth required. Anne had sent them out together to spend time on a longer walk, not because of any need she had.

But Elizabeth could forgive her matchmaking friend very easily, as it had been instructive to see Mr. Darcy's dealings with the others here, so very different from his behaviour in Meryton. She wished she could know what it meant. Was Mr. Darcy the man she had met in Hertfordshire, who was haughty, superior, and meddling? Or was he the man by her side, the honourable man who saw to everyone's problems but never made a promise he could not keep?

She hoped the man she was seeing today was the man he truly was, and in her heart, she believed that he was. After all, the men who had come to speak with him thought so, as did Miss Addison. What daughter of a tenant would be comfortable asking such a boon from a man who was only related to the mistress of the estate?

Elizabeth knew the answer to that. Because she trusted him to be kind. She stepped back outside.

"It is a fine letter," Mr. Darcy told her. "The colonel has authorized me to act on his behalf in this matter. Would you like to walk over to the post now and send it? They should have a seal."

"I would," she replied, and Mr. Darcy offered her his arm.

She took it.

Elizabeth knew why Miss Addison had sought out Mr. Darcy. Because he would act when Lady Catherine might not. She looked over at the tall, handsome man from Derbyshire and decided that she could wait to think about this new, surprising Mr. Darcy.

For now, it was simply pleasant to walk with him.

When Darcy returned to Rosings, having delivered Miss Elizabeth's letter to the post and Miss Elizabeth to the parsonage, an acrid odour made him glance up. Thick black smoke rising from the eastern side of the estate propelled Darcy around the side of the great house and out to the stables.

"My horse! And inform Colonel Fitzwilliam . . ."

"He's out on a ride, Mr. Darcy," the groom said, bringing Darcy's horse, already saddled. "Shall we load up the cart to bring water?"

"Quick as you can."

Darcy took the reins of the horse and wheeled about before he urged his mount into a full run.

It was nearly two miles to the site, even using the narrow path through the trees. Mr. Salter and his family lived here—he leased one of the larger farms. Darcy nearly threw himself from the saddle, but before he could utter a single order, he saw that a group of about ten men from the other tenant farms were already there, using a nearby well to pass buckets of water up to the front of two lines.

Fitzwilliam was one of the men running with the buckets and dumping the water on the flames, wearing an expression of determination and purpose. This must be how he appeared to his soldiers.

"We have it now, men!" he shouted, and there was a spirited cheer from those assembled.

A woman with several small children, faces covered in soot, was sitting a short distance away while the men worked to put out what remained of the fire. One part of the cottage was a loss, but most of the structure could be saved. The fire was nearly out already, though Darcy was not sorry that more water was on its way. It was best to drown the embers, and they could all use it to wash up, if nothing else.

Fitzwilliam dumped a last bucket and then spied Darcy. He lifted a hand and relinquished his place to the man behind him. "Darcy! If you are come to offer assistance, you are a little late. Spent a bit too much time walking with the charming Miss Bennet?"

The others chuckled a bit. Even in the face of a fire, apparently his pursuit of Miss Elizabeth was entertainment for them all. "I was only just walking back to the house. I had quite a few questions to answer for those in town."

"You can bring them to me when I have cleaned up," Fitzwilliam informed him, then gestured behind him. "The kitchen went up. It appears the children were playing where they ought not to have been. But no one was hurt, and we stopped the flames from taking the entire house."

"It is fortunate you were nearby," Darcy said. Quite without thinking, he added, "I will handle the requests, if you prefer. They are nothing I have not done before."

"That would be a great help," Fitzwilliam replied. "I tell you, this sort of thing gets the blood going, but learning the habit of sitting at a desk for hours with no chance of activity—that has little appeal to me."

Unfortunately, sitting at a desk was a more regular duty than fighting fires. "There is more water coming," Darcy informed him.

"Thank you, Darcy," Fitzwilliam said, and returned to the group of men who had helped put out the blaze.

"When you men have done," a woman he recognised as Mrs. Pattison called, "we will see whether any of the clothing or other goods might be saved with a good washing. Then I'll take Cassie and the children home."

"Aye," replied Mr. Pattison. He swiped an arm across his forehead.

There was nothing for him to do here. Fitzwilliam was seeing to it all.

He walked over to Mrs. Salter and crouched down to speak with her where she sat on a stump, her children hanging about her. "Are you and your children well? May I provide anything for your relief?"

The lean, spare woman gazed at him, both fatigue and fright in her eyes. "No, sir, I thank you. We are all well, and the Millers have said we can stay with them until the house is fixed."

"Very well. Should you require anything, just send someone up to the house." He glanced back at Fitzwilliam. "One of us will ride out tomorrow to see about the repairs."

She nodded. "Thank you, sir."

Darcy wandered back to the men and heard the rumble of the cart from Rosings coming around on the road. He rubbed the back of his neck.

Fitzwilliam would be fine, if he could ever find a way to appreciate the more mundane duties of the estate. Whether or not his cousin was willing to do so, however, remained a mystery.

Chapter Eight

"What seems to be the problem, Darcy?" Fitzwilliam asked with a sly smile. "Here it is Friday already. Are you so busy courting that you allow your business to go untended?"

Darcy sighed. He *had* been thinking primarily of Miss Elizabeth these past days, but something had also been bothering him about Fitzwilliam. "I have seen to the most pressing matters, and I have not *promised* anything other than to Miss Addison. I told her we would pay the apothecary to tend her father."

"But you spoke with several other men?"

"Yes. The grocer, the butcher, the Grenvilles who lease the farm . . ."

"I know where the Grenville farm is, Darcy. What do you think I was doing on my ride before the fire?"

He had thought Fitzwilliam on a pleasure ride, truth be told. His cousin often rode when he felt hemmed in. "Have you spoken with Barnaby yet?"

Fitzwilliam shook his head. "I have not decided whether I will or not. Perhaps it is best to play this off as though I did not notice but not allow it to be repeated."

That was not the right way to go about it. "Or he might spend the next quarter bragging about fooling you into paying him more than he was due and encouraging others to attempt the same."

Fitzwilliam sighed. "Really, Darcy, what happened to allowing me to learn from my mistakes? What would you have me do?"

Darcy had not wanted to assist further with this, but it was a small matter in the face of the other issues to be resolved. "Send a letter no later than tomorrow morning, explaining that there has been a discrepancy and you will be deducting the two pounds from his next payment."

Fitzwilliam stared at him. "That easy?"

"Not everything must be complex."

"Fine. *You* write the letter."

"In addition to contacting the others I spoke to in the village? It is not my estate, cousin. It will soon be yours."

"It is Anne's."

"Yours together, then."

Fitzwilliam scoffed. "You do not believe I can do it." He shook his head tiredly. "Perhaps you are right. Write the letter to Barnaby. I am sure it will be better, coming from you."

Darcy frowned. "Your competence has never been at issue."

"Then what?"

"It is just . . ." he hesitated.

"*What?*" Fitzwilliam ground out.

Darcy blew out a long breath. He had learned *something* from his experience with Miss Elizabeth. "Nothing."

Fitzwilliam stood and leaned over the desk in a manner that might have cowed any young officer but did not intimidate him.

"Darcy," he said, nearly growling, "tell me what is on your mind. I am too tired to beat it out of you tonight."

Darcy grinned. "As if you could, *Richie*."

His cousin actually growled, and Darcy threw up his hands. "Fine," he said with a bit of a laugh and then grew sombre. "I do not doubt your abilities. I never have. But I do . . . I am sorry to say it, but I do doubt your commitment."

Fitzwilliam's stare was as cold as a snowy January in Derbyshire. He reached into a drawer for some paper and handed it to Darcy with a pen. Then he uncorked the ink. "Fine. Write everything down, and I will see to it. Eventually you will have to leave for London, and I will need to know what you said."

Darcy did not take up the pen. "Will you not be accompanying me?"

"Only long enough to submit my resignation and draw up a marriage contract. Then I shall return here."

Finally, Darcy recognized what was causing his own disquiet. "So you do still plan to marry Anne?"

Fitzwilliam narrowed his eyes. "Did you think I would not?"

"That is not an answer."

Darcy's cousin looked away.

"You were uncomfortable with the proposal from the first," Darcy said. "Did you even believe that Anne would accept it?"

Fitzwilliam closed his eyes and sighed. "No. And she should not have. I am not the right man for Rosings."

"You have not even tried! Not with the estate *or* Anne."

"I have!" Fitzwilliam insisted.

Darcy sighed with exasperation. "You mucked around in the paperwork without any plan or sense of organization, and you made a half-hearted attempt with Barnaby that might have cost you not only two pounds but made Rosings a target for cheats. Two or three pertinent questions about quarterly payments and how the accounts are paid would have prevented the error, yet you were determined not to speak with me about it." He frowned. "I am the one working with Houseman to negotiate the land purchase with the Botterills and you also want me to deal with the questions I encountered in town. Despite all of that, I have been spending every available moment with Miss Bennet, attempting to know her better. You have barely met with Houseman and hardly spent any time at all with Anne, to whom you are actually engaged."

"I know Anne far better than you know Miss Bennet."

"Do you? How much time have you spent at Rosings in the last several years? Even now you are out riding or closed in here, where I suspect you are busier drinking wine than reviewing the accounts." He felt a little ill. "Do you even want to marry Anne?"

Fitzwilliam closed his eyes and avoided answering. "The problem is that I am a soldier, Darcy. I know so little about running an estate. Can I do what is required?"

"You can. Houseman will not lead you wrong, and I am always available if you have questions he cannot address. Is that all?"

Fitzwilliam looked up. "I simply cannot reconcile having such good fortune when I have failed Anne so miserably."

"What do you mean?" Darcy inquired, thoroughly confused.

His cousin shook his head. "Wickham should never have been alone with her."

Darcy was incredulous. "You mean the summer at Pemberley? That was ten years ago, cousin! Anne had a companion, and we were both little more than boys. How were we to know?"

"I should have been able to do more than break the miscreant's nose, Darcy. How he remained in the family, so close to your father, was criminal."

"My father was a good man," Darcy said with a sigh, "but he had much to answer for in his dealings with George Wickham." He poured them both a glass of port, and they drank in silence for a time. Eventually, Darcy asked the question he had been wondering all along. "Why did you shove Anne and I apart, Fitzwilliam?"

His cousin laid his head against the window and looked out across the garden. "I have said before, I do not know!"

"Did you believe you were saving me from proposing to a woman who did not want me?"

Fitzwilliam shrugged half-heartedly. "Perhaps."

"If that was your concern, I thank you for your trouble, though it was hardly necessary. I am simply trying to offer you the same consideration." Darcy hesitated, but then forged ahead. "Fitzwilliam, you have said that you will marry Anne. Very good. But if you cannot *love* her . . ." He hesitated, but determined he must forge ahead. "I beg you, do not wed her."

Darcy did not wish the wedding to be abandoned. He cared deeply for both of his cousins. But that was precisely the point, was it not? Anne was happy now, but if she learned—and eventually, she would—that her husband felt trapped because he had panicked and blurted out a proposal he did not expect her to accept, she would be devastated. They would both be forced to live with that knowledge for the rest of their lives. He watched, his heart heavy, as Fitzwilliam began to pace around the room.

After many minutes of silent agitation, Fitzwilliam asked in an icy tone, "What are you saying?"

"Only this," Darcy said, with every appearance of calm, though he was far from complacent. "If you do not love her like a husband should, Fitz—do not wed her. For you shall break her heart and you shall both of you be unhappy without any way to remedy your situation."

Fitzwilliam shook his head. "You doubt my commitment," he said, echoing Darcy's words from earlier. "I do not suppose I can blame you for that. No, I gave my word, and I mean to fulfil it."

"Speak with Anne, Fitzwilliam. Perhaps together . . ."

"No more of your platitudes, Darcy. Just leave me be. I must think."

"Very well," Darcy agreed. He set down his glass and moved to the door. There was nothing more he could do.

Chapter Nine

On Friday, Elizabeth received two letters. One was from Papa, who had responded to her warning with what was, for him, surprising haste. She read his brief note quickly, and was disheartened, though not surprised. He had seen an opportunity to sport with her—that was the reason for his prompt attention. She tucked it away to think about later.

After she seated herself at the breakfast table to await the others, Elizabeth broke the seal on Jane's letter and read it through carefully. She smiled to herself and then read it again with increasing delight. Mr. Bingley had called at Gracechurch Street and apologised for the manner in which he had removed from Netherfield.

He thought me indifferent, Lizzy. Can you imagine? I disabused him at once, and he was so very pleased. Oh, Lizzy! He is to come again today. How shall I bear so much happiness?

This letter from Jane, combined with her stroll into the village with Mr. Darcy, had satisfied nearly the last of her concerns—that he was on his best behaviour only because he wished her to see him in a good light. The idea that others saw him as trustworthy offered her much relief.

So many people came to Mr. Darcy for help even here in Kent, where he spent only a few weeks a year and was not the master of the estate, that he must have a reputation for trustworthiness. And the way he had dealt with poor Miss Addison, who had summoned all her boldness to speak with him on behalf of her father, was encouraging. Any man might grant Miss Addison's need for charity and send her on her way. But Elizabeth could not deny that there had been a good deal more in Mr. Darcy's manner. He had been politely formal with the gentlemen, but he had shown the girl genuine kindness.

However, while his performance in town had put one doubt to rest, it had raised another. Unlike Elizabeth's father, Mr. Darcy took charge of every situation that required it—and perhaps others that did not. What continued to bother her was the notion that even when well-intentioned, Mr. Darcy was so certain of his course that he did not allow for other opinions.

She had a great many opinions. Any husband of hers would need to be willing to acquiesce to *some* of them.

If Papa would gladly pass off anything that required effort to someone else willing to do it, Mr. Darcy was the man who took on everything from those who did not wish to do the work. Was he not still working with Mr. Houseman and speaking for the estate despite the fact that the colonel would soon be the master of Rosings? Should Mr. Darcy not be teaching Anne's intended how to run the estate on his own rather than continuing to act as master himself?

He was a man of extraordinary diligence, it was true, but such devotion created its own problems. First, he would exhaust himself taking care of everything rather than allowing others to help him. He was a young man now, but he would not always be, and when would he find time to spend with his wife and family? Second, it had the potential to make those around him either lazy or resentful, and Elizabeth counted herself among the latter.

Charlotte and Maria finally entered the breakfast room followed by Mr. Collins. Maria filled her plate and sat to eat. She was never very lively before the morning meal.

"How is your courtship with Mr. Darcy proceeding, Eliza?" Charlotte asked once she took her place at one end of the table. "Well, I hope."

"Well enough, Charlotte, thank you."

"Please, Mrs. Collins," her husband said with a bit of a grunt as he examined the food, "let us speak of pleasanter things."

"I find it very pleasant to consider the possibility of Mr. Darcy marrying our cousin and becoming a part of our family, Mr. Collins," Charlotte replied easily. "Do you not?"

Mr. Collins's expression pinched as he worked out his wife's meaning. Like the sun gradually lifting above the horizon to dispel the dark, his expression transformed. "I had not thought of that," he admitted, and for once, there were no words to follow.

"Come sit with us, husband," Charlotte said sweetly, and poured out a cup of coffee. She handed it to Mr. Collins, who took it gratefully in one hand while placing down his plate with the other. Then he sat in a chair that moaned under his weight, for he was nearly as tall as Mr. Darcy, but half again as wide. He was not corpulent, but tending that way, and Charlotte's excellent table was unlikely to make him any thinner.

"Thank you, Mrs. Collins" was all he said.

Charlotte had worked a miracle. Elizabeth shot her a questioning look, but her friend simply smiled and lifted a cup of tea to her lips.

Elizabeth had to confess, even if only to herself, that she looked forward to seeing Mr. Darcy, for though she enjoyed visiting with Anne and helping her prepare for her wedding, the walk back and forth from Rosings this past week had become the best part of her day. Not that she could tell Charlotte as much until she was completely certain how she wished this courtship to end—with an amicable if unsatisfying parting, or a visit to her father.

"Good day, Miss Elizabeth," Mr. Darcy said in his sonorous voice when she stepped out into the hall a half-hour later to greet him. She returned the greeting, then gathered her bonnet and gloves.

"Anne is not quite ready for your visit, she informs me," Mr. Darcy said once they were in the lane. "But she suggested I arrive at my usual time and show you something of the gardens. I did not remind her I already had."

"She really is just as scheming as her mother, is she not?" Elizabeth was amused.

"My cousin is better at it, truth be told. Lady Catherine only demands, Anne . . . offers opportunities."

Elizabeth laughed at the peculiar expression on his countenance as he struggled to come up with the politest way of saying that Anne had perhaps invested herself too much in their relationship.

"Well, then, Mr. Darcy. Which garden shall we visit?"

"Ah," he said lightly. "It is not a garden, precisely. But you shall have to wait, for it is a surprise."

"Come, Mr. Darcy. Have I not seen every field and glade that one can without riding?"

"I do not believe so," he said ambiguously.

It piqued Elizabeth's curiosity. Dreadful man, he must have known it would.

Whatever he was thinking, he had been correct. Elizabeth had to admit, as they went over a small rise and then took a sharp left around it and walked up another hill, that she had never taken this path before. They entered a large grove of trees with nothing but a slender path wending through it. He took hold of a thorny branch from a wild blackberry bush and bent it back until she had walked past. Once she had, he carefully released it and turned to her.

"Close your eyes, Miss Elizabeth," he said.

"Really, Mr. Darcy, must I?"

"Yes." That was the taciturn man she recalled, but then chided herself for being a spoilsport and shut her eyes tight.

"Are they closed?"

She felt the air stir near her face. Was he really waving his hand before her eyes to be certain they were closed?

Well, he might be right to do so. She *had* been known to peek.

Mr. Darcy took her arm and led her carefully forward. By the time the rays of the sun warmed her upturned face, Elizabeth was wild to know where Mr. Darcy was leading her.

"Miss Elizabeth," he said near her ear, and at the sound of her name on his lips Elizabeth trembled with an emotion she could not name. "Open your eyes."

Before her was an ocean of yellow tulips bathed in sunlight, surrounded by green grasses and a brilliant blue sky. The tulips, hundreds of them, nodded gracefully in the breeze. She gasped at the splendour of it, raising her hands to her chest and clasping them together in delight. "Oh, Mr. Darcy, it is magnificent!"

"Normally," Mr. Darcy said quietly, "I am a proponent of leaving nature to do its work whenever possible. But every year, my aunt has this field planted in memory of Sir Lewis. The yellow tulip was his favourite flower."

Elizabeth was overwhelmed by the beauty of the field and the sentiment behind it. No wonder the tulips were planted in this rather private spot. It was meant to be a place of reflection. "They were married for ten years, I understand."

"Nearly eleven, and, I am told, very much in love. Sir Lewis was some years older than my aunt, but it was still a surprise to us all that he died when he did. He was not an aged man and had seemed quite healthy."

"I own I am a little surprised that Lady Catherine never remarried. She must have still been quite young."

"My father once remarked that she feared a new husband might decide to send Anne away, and that she would not allow it."

"Send Anne away?"

"Yes, Sir Lewis was a widower with a daughter when he and my aunt married."

"Do you think that might have happened?"

"Possibly. But I also knew, even at my tender age, that my aunt loved my uncle a great deal. It is just as likely that she was not interested in marrying anyone else." They stood in silence a moment before he added, "She has been widowed now longer than she was wed."

"I am sorry for her, then. And for you all. Does Anne have no other blood relations?"

"Only some distant de Bourgh cousins who did not want her. Sir Lewis was not a favourite among them, you see, for not only had he married the daughter of a Whig, he gave her the right to live in the manor house at Rosings for the rest of her life."

Elizabeth shook her head. "Fortunate for Lady Catherine, for she would have had no standing if the de Bourghs had wished to claim Anne as their own." She gazed out over the field and smiled up at him. "Thank you for bringing me here."

Darcy nodded. "I had considered a bouquet, but I suspected you would appreciate this more."

Her heart swelled with some unknowable emotion at how well he had understood this facet of her character. Elizabeth preferred to leave flowers growing when she could, for she could enjoy them longer that way.

"Yes," she told him. "You were quite right. You have given me flowers and a walk." She gestured towards the field. "Just look at the size of it!"

"The first year, my aunt had one hundred bulbs planted. She has added to it since."

Elizabeth chuckled. "That much is obvious. Must it be replanted each year?"

Darcy shook his head. "Tulips will grow again if tended properly. It is only when the flowers begin to lose their vitality that the gardeners remove them."

Elizabeth nodded. "Does your aunt come here when the flowers are in bloom?"

"She does. She had a bench built . . . there." He gestured to the other end of the field, where a small bench was located under the shade of a tree. "She does not like to visit his grave, so she sits there instead. She is a forceful woman, but I sometimes walk here to remember that she is also a loving one."

Elizabeth understood requiring such an aid to his memory, for Lady Catherine was more than forceful. But perhaps there were reasons for that. She stared at the tulips and wished she knew how to paint. Alas, the glorious vision would have to remain no more than a pleasant memory.

Mr. Darcy took a deep breath and released it as he gazed out upon the field of flowers. "There is something steadying about natural beauty," he murmured, glancing at Elizabeth.

"I quite agree, Mr. Darcy." She offered him an impish smile. "Are you surprised that I am agreeing with you without persuasion?"

He smiled. "I know you often assert beliefs not your own in the service of a debate."

Was he calling her a liar? She saw from his smile that he was teasing her. "A debate? Or an argument?"

"Probably a bit of both."

Elizabeth laughed. "You do know how to offer compliments to a lady, Mr. Darcy."

"Certainly I do. I have been to the very best schools, Miss Bennet," Mr. Darcy said haughtily, but then smiled again. "I am afraid, however, that the curriculum did not cover how to please a woman worthy of being pleased." He leaned forward, and Elizabeth's heart began to dance wildly in her chest. He slipped one large hand under hers and lifted it to his lips.

It was very bold. It was also very effective, for Elizabeth felt her cheeks burning, and knew not what to say.

"Have I rendered you speechless, Miss Bennet?" he teased, still holding her hand.

"I suppose," Elizabeth managed to reply, "you believed that such was not possible."

"I had not, to tell the truth. You are so rarely caught off guard."

"This is too much flattery, Mr. Darcy."

"No," he insisted, "I do not flatter you." His expression was almost boyish when he said, "By now you must be aware that I do not know how."

"You may have been keeping it a secret." She arched one eyebrow, and Mr. Darcy responded by rolling his eyes. He finally released his hold, and Elizabeth wished that he had not.

"You know my family," he replied. "How likely is that?"

"*You* know how to keep secrets, though," she said pointedly, and he nodded.

"I do, when it is important. But I would not expect to have secrets from my . . ."

"Your what, Mr. Darcy?"

He leaned in to say, very quietly, "My wife, Miss Bennet."

A pleasant shiver travelled down Elizabeth's spine. "Are you making a request, sir?"

Mr. Darcy pulled back slowly and studied her before saying, "Not yet. Not until I am quite certain the woman I mean to ask will be able to offer me the answer I seek."

"And you do not think she is?"

He gazed at her, and Elizabeth felt it again, as she had when they spoke in the hall outside of Anne's sitting room. There was something quietly magnetic in his presence, and it was all there to be read in his eyes. That she had not been able to understand it before was now quite incomprehensible to her.

"No," he said at last. "Not quite yet."

Chapter Ten

Elizabeth was a little piqued when they at last made their way to the little yellow sitting room where Anne awaited her. How much had changed in a week's time! She had fully expected Mr. Darcy to propose again, not to put her off. Elizabeth wanted to say yes to him. She thought she did.

She stepped inside and turned to thank Mr. Darcy.

"Miss Bennet, it was a pleasure. Anne," Mr. Darcy said, and bowed.

Just as Elizabeth was about to bid farewell to him, Anne closed the door firmly in his face and turned the lock.

"Anne?"

Anne's eyes were rimmed with red, and she was gasping as tears rolled down her flushed cheeks.

Alarm made her grasp Anne's arm. "Whatever is the matter?"

"He does not want us to marry!"

It was nearly a wail, the words nearly indistinguishable and the sound so loud that it must have pierced even Mr. Darcy's calm façade.

"Anne?" Mr. Darcy called through the door. He knocked twice and raised his voice. "Anne?"

Elizabeth was confused. "Who does not want you to marry?"

"Darcy!" Anne sobbed. "He begged Richard not to marry me! And Richard said nothing!"

"What?" The word burst from Elizabeth before she could stop it. "Why? Did he say?"

"Miss Elizabeth, would you be so kind as to open the door?" Mr. Darcy asked, his alarm clear in the request.

Anne sniffed. "I was going to knock on the study door and ask to join them. We have spent much time together on this visit, all three of us. But before I could, I heard Darcy beg Richard not to marry me."

"I cannot believe it," Elizabeth breathed. "What did the colonel say?"

"He said nothing! Nothing at all! I waited for several minutes before I fled back upstairs. I have been waiting for you here ever since."

"Would someone please inform me what is happening?" Mr. Darcy asked gruffly, and then Elizabeth heard another male voice in the hall. The colonel had come.

"She is weeping," she heard Mr. Darcy say, his deep, agitated voice carrying, and then, "I do not *know* why, Fitzwilliam. They are in there, and I am out here."

Mr. Darcy had never really said he was wrong to interfere with Jane and Mr. Bingley, had he? Only that his understanding was faulty. Elizabeth chewed her bottom lip. Was this not the precise thing she was worried about with him? That he could feel himself entitled to interfere in the affairs of everyone else without thought or concern for the consequences? That he was so used to having his own way that he could do such terribly insensitive, intrusive things like this without thought?

Had she allowed a few romantic walks to sway her judgment?

Elizabeth grasped the back of a chair. She felt a little dizzy. Anne leaned into her, her tears wetting Elizabeth's shoulder, and she patted her friend's back while her own sentiments moved from anger to irritation to betrayal.

It felt an age before she shook herself into sense again, though it must only have been a few minutes. One thing her father had taught her was to examine her feelings when they confused her, and when she did, there was a question she was forced to ask herself.

What judgement?

She closed her eyes and saw before her hundreds of yellow tulips, Mr. Darcy removing a thorny branch from her path without ceremony, his quiet expression of pleasure each time he arrived to walk with her. Not only that. How had he treated Miss Addison as she begged for assistance? How he had tended to Anne as she arrived, breathless, at the parsonage?

She had been wrong about Mr. Wickham. She had been wrong about Anne. She had even been wrong about her father. Papa loved her, that she was sure of. But he did not respect her.

Not like Mr. Darcy did.

Anne pulled away with an apology, and Elizabeth handed her a hand-kerchief. As Anne wandered to the settee and nearly threw herself upon it, Elizabeth placed her hand against her chest, trying to still the panic that was making her heart race at a sickening speed. This was the very last of her fears, was it not? She was afraid that her wishes or opinions would be ignored, afraid to be treated as her father dealt with her mother. But the marriage of Uncle and Aunt Gardiner proved it did not have to be that way, and Mr. Darcy had shown that he respected her opinions. Had he not agreed that her sisters must be warned against Mr. Wickham, even at the risk of exposing his family's private dealings with the man? Even though he was perhaps the most private man she had ever known?

The fact that the man she loved would be imperfect was something she had known, intellectually, for as long as she had considered marriage. No one was perfect. Even the Gardiners had their little quarrels. Elizabeth had truly believed she understood and could make allowances for that—she was hardly a paragon of perfection herself. Still, the reality of those imperfections in the person of Mr. Darcy had been more difficult to contend with.

Elizabeth smiled wryly at her ruminations and considered that she had been a girl last autumn and that she was perhaps nearer a woman now. Mr. Darcy had made amends as far as he was able. It was time to truly release the last of her girlish petulance at his performance last autumn, as she had promised she would. She would trust him as much as he evidently trusted her.

He loved her, had he not said as much in the parsonage? He had. And she . . .

She felt the same.

It took a little more time to collect herself, for she must first chastise herself for doubting Mr. Darcy. But eventually, she was ready.

"We should request the men join us and insist they explain," she said firmly. Surely there was a rational explanation. Mr. Darcy could not have arranged to show her Lady Catherine's tulips—such a lovely surprise—and at the very same time be scheming to disrupt his cousins' engagement.

"I cannot," Anne said, and buried her face in her hands. "I am so humiliated."

Elizabeth stepped to the door.

"Do not open the door, Elizabeth!" Anne cried.

"I will not invite them in," Elizabeth replied, "but we must stop them from entering despite us, for they are aware you are distressed." She turned the knob and peeked out into the hall, where two very concerned-looking young men were standing no more than a foot away. "You must allow me a little time to speak with Anne, gentlemen. Please be patient."

"I do not understand—what has happened?" the colonel inquired hastily.

Elizabeth pressed her lips together. She could not help but glance at Mr. Darcy before she said, "Anne has overheard something that has dismayed her, that is all."

"Let me speak with her," the colonel said, reaching for the knob. "I would like to help, if I may."

"I am sorry to say that the two of you are the source of her disquiet. Please, allow me to speak with her first."

"Miss Bennet," Mr. Darcy said quietly. "What is the matter?"

"She overheard something about her engagement, Mr. Darcy. Something that displeased her." Elizabeth was gentle in her remonstrance. She only meant to offer them a clue and was heartened when they both appeared bemused by her statement. Suddenly the colonel's head turned sharply to regard his cousin, and in the shocked silence that followed, Elizabeth shut the door.

"Lock it!" Anne cried. She held a sodden handkerchief pressed to her eyes.

Elizabeth did as she was asked, but no sooner had she removed the key than she was startled by the sound of someone pounding a fist against the wood on the other side.

"Anne, let me in!" the colonel exclaimed. "I can explain! I can explain it all!"

"I will not have you forced to marry me, Richard," Anne called back hotly, and turned her back. "Stupid man," she told Elizabeth pulling her to the other side of the room. "I was so sure he loved me. Why else would he have acted as he did in the parsonage?" She crossed her arms over her chest.

Elizabeth shook her head. "Why would Mr. Darcy have acted as *he* did at the parsonage, so quickly offering to remedy his mistake with Mr. Bingley and my sister, only to interfere in the engagement between the two of you?"

Anne stopped and peered at Elizabeth quizzically. "You do not believe that he would do so only to make you believe he has changed?"

That was not what Elizabeth had meant. She had been attempting to point out that such behaviour on the part of Mr. Darcy would have been inconsistent. He was many things, but not a hypocrite. She began to believe he was the best man she had ever known.

To her dismay, Elizabeth began to cry.

She wept for her foolishness in taking the side of Mr. Wickham when Mr. Darcy had been everything honourable to a man who had already betrayed him—and then betrayed him a second time. Seeing him so respected in the village made her proud of him. And today—he had put forth such an effort to show her something beautiful, something he knew she would enjoy . . . no, it was not that he had put forth the effort, not that alone. She was impressed and pleased because Mr. Darcy knew her well enough to take her on a walk to a field of tulips rather than send her flowers from the garden for her chambers. He was thoughtful. She might even say he was romantic. Her temples throbbed. Oh, how blind she had been!

"Elizabeth?" Anne asked, thoroughly diverted from her own complaints. "I did not mean that *I* believed it! I am only anxious that *you* do. Please do not cry."

Elizabeth quieted and sniffed. "I am a wretched friend, Anne, indulging myself in such a crisis of spirit when in your company."

"True," Anne told her pertly. "For I was having one first." She held out Elizabeth's handkerchief. "I fear it is already damp."

Elizabeth took it and they both laughed softly through their tears.

"Should we allow them in?" Elizabeth asked anxiously.

"Never mind them," Anne said, waving her hand. "They can wait. They deserve to stand out there for another hour at least. First, tell me, why are *you* crying?"

"It is only that I am vexed," Elizabeth said, dabbing at her eyes with the cloth.

"The men in this family would try the patience of a saint," Anne agreed with a huff and fell into a chair in a pet. "What did Darcy do?"

"Why do you think it is something Mr. Darcy has done?"

Anne sighed. "Elizabeth," she said, exasperated. "It is *Darcy*."

Elizabeth waved a hand between Anne and the door. "It is not Mr. Darcy, as it happens, but my own treatment of him."

"Oh," Anne responded, and frowned. "Truly?"

"I am afraid I have not dealt fairly with him." Elizabeth admitted. "And though he has often been wrong, so have I. Now that we have reconciled, he deserves my trust and respect and I am determined to offer it to him. Anne, are you *sure* he has attempted to break your engagement? What could possibly be his reasoning? It seems nonsensical, given everything he has done recently."

"As to that, my family does nonsensical things all the time, Elizabeth," Anne said plainly. "Does not yours?" She lifted her shoulders. "Darcy is clever in many ways, but when it comes to people who do not depend upon him for their livelihood, he is a bit of a . . ."

"Dolt?" Elizabeth asked teasingly, remembering that Anne had previously used that word to describe Mr. Darcy.

"Yes. Precisely. Dolts, the pair of them. Here, sit down." She motioned to an overstuffed chair, one of a pair set by the hearth, and Elizabeth sat by her.

"I must apologise," Anne said, taking Elizabeth's hands in her own. "I did not think how you would respond to my temper, for I am not really upset with Darcy. I was only thinking of Richard's silence. Has he learned nothing in all these years?"

"Whatever do you mean?"

"I mean . . ." although she had only just insisted they sit, Anne stood abruptly and brushed her hands down her skirt. "Well, we must speak to our dolts, no? There is no comprehending them until we speak to them, you are quite right."

It was not precisely what Elizabeth had said, nor had she meant it, but in this she believed it best to allow Anne her way.

Darcy was certain he had heard Miss Elizabeth weeping right along with Anne, though he could not hear what they said. He had been left to cool his heels in the hallway with Fitzwilliam and the wait was excruciating.

If the waiting did not kill him, Fitzwilliam might. Darcy's cousin was standing entirely still, his arms crossed over his chest, facing the door to Anne's sitting room as though he might be able to bore a hole in the wood if he stared at it hard enough. The servants had long since slunk away, not wishing to be about when they were both in such a state. Darcy could not blame them.

"This is your fault, Darcy," Fitzwilliam grumbled, without turning his head.

"We do not even know what is happening. How can you know it is my fault?"

"Because of the two of us, I am not the one who makes women cry."

He had Darcy there. Fitzwilliam was all charm and affability. Darcy was . . . not.

"Might we wait for them to inform us precisely what has happened before you lay all the blame at my feet?"

"You know what they heard, Darcy. Miss Elizabeth said as much. You told me not to marry Anne. She must have heard you pose the question and then left while I was still walking around the study trying to pull my thoughts together."

"Clearly she did not hear everything." Darcy scratched the back of his head and recalled his words to Fitzwilliam. "Though I admit, it would sound terrible if that is the only portion of the conversation she managed to overhear," he admitted.

"An understatement if there ever was one," Fitzwilliam spat out. "Not unlike separating Bingley from her sister."

"That was an entirely different situation."

"I doubt Miss Bennet sees it as such."

Ludicrous. Miss Elizabeth could not feel that this was the same . . . but he stopped himself. He was used to simply dismissing things he knew to be false, but if someone as intelligent as Miss Elizabeth required an explanation, then perhaps he was wrong to do so.

Though he had sensed this morning that she was not ready to receive his offer, he had thought them very close after the tulips. No, he could not dismiss Elizabeth's concerns if he ever hoped to make her happy, both now, and eventually, as his wife. And he did want her happy. More than he wanted it for himself.

That hope had been somewhat dampened by the time Anne opened the door nearly an hour after she had shut it. Fitzwilliam had been ready to seek out the housekeeper and insist that she give him the key, but if he had, Lady Catherine would have been alerted and this entire episode would have been made a hundred times worse.

"Come," Anne said in that direct, plain-speaking manner of hers, and turned her back as she retreated to the far side of the room.

Fitzwilliam strode purposefully after Anne, and Darcy stepped in behind him before closing the door. It was not proper, of course, but he refused to bend to propriety when everything he desired was in this room and might be slipping through his fingers. They were not alone. It was enough. He glanced over at Anne and Fitzwilliam, but Miss Elizabeth was not on that side of the chamber. Turning, he spied her in the opposite corner near two stuffed chairs.

She was looking out the window, in the direction of the hillside where the tulips were planted, though they were not visible from here. Her arms were wrapped around her narrow waist.

He approached to stand just behind her and to one side, his hands clasped together behind his back to keep himself under good regulation. For a moment, he watched her reflection in the glass.

"You would never know that the tulips were there, just on the other side of the slope," she said without looking at him.

"It is the way my aunt prefers it," Darcy replied, wondering whether she was saying something entirely different to him. "She mourns him still, but not in public."

Miss Elizabeth took a breath so deep that her shoulders rose. "There is so much beneath the surface with you, Mr. Darcy. I am trying to make you out."

"A lifetime's occupation, madam."

She closed her eyes and sighed. "That is not an exaggeration."

His heart thumped painfully in his chest. "Then we are in exactly the same situation, Miss Bennet, for I never know what you will do next." He shrugged, something he had never thought to do in the presence of a lady. "I should never have thought you would be so troubled about what Anne overheard."

"Not troubled!" she cried, whirling about to face him. "However, I am ashamed to say that I rushed to a hasty conclusion. Again. But I have learnt my lesson and wish to discuss this with you before I pronounce that judgement sound."

"I am grateful that you are seeking confirmation," Darcy told her gently, remembering their promise to one another to do just that. "First, we must ascertain whether we are discussing the same thing, for Anne could not have heard the entire conversation or she would not have shut us out."

That made Miss Elizabeth smile a bit before she said, seriously, "Anne heard you beg the colonel not to marry her. You have done so before, and I am sorry to say I feared it might be true."

Darcy frowned. He reached for her hands, and although the furrows in her forehead suggested she was conflicted, Miss Elizabeth allowed the liberty. "I would never step between my cousins. I have learnt my lesson."

"What *did* you say, Mr. Darcy? Be precise, if you will, for I feel there must be some great mistake on Anne's part."

Darcy gazed at Miss Elizabeth fondly. She was waiting for his explanation. She *wished* to think the best of him. This was progress indeed. "I told Fitzwilliam that he should not marry Anne *if he could not love her*."

"You . . . what?" She blinked up at him, bemused.

"Fitzwilliam," Darcy called across the room, "what did I tell you in the study?"

His cousin repeated what he had just told Miss Elizabeth, then scowled at Darcy and returned to speaking earnestly with Anne in tones too low to be discerned.

Darcy explained the entire conversation. "Given the way in which Fitzwilliam made his offer, I was concerned. He worried Anne had accepted him for the wrong reasons, and given his ambivalence about taking on the estate work here, I could not be certain of his state of mind. I do not love Anne as more than a cousin, but over the years I have seen that love is what she wants most of all."

Elizabeth nodded. "Anne was sure the colonel loved her even though he had not said as much."

"She is wiser than either of us, then. Fortunately, I think Fitzwilliam is finally prepared to admit that he loves Anne and that he is fully capable of being a good husband to her. He was in agony waiting out in the hall. As was I, when I heard your tears. May I ask why . . . ?"

"I was disappointed," Miss Elizabeth confessed.

"With me?"

She shook her head. "With myself."

"Why in the world would you be upset with yourself?" She truly was a complex creature.

"Just for a moment, I believed you had interfered with your cousins' engagement in the same way you did with Jane and Mr. Bingley. I allowed myself to doubt you after I had promised to exonerate you there."

"I am pleased to hear it," Darcy replied, grateful that he had risen so high in her esteem. He could not help himself, however, and added, "Of course, Bingley was never engaged to your sister."

Her huff was adorable. "Immaterial, Mr. Darcy. Was not that the substance of your discussion with Mr. Bingley? That he ought not marry her?"

"Can you truly see no difference between the two?"

Miss Elizabeth's countenance paled. She had not thought it that far through, apparently, but to her credit, she did so now, and while he waited for her to finish, Darcy entertained himself by observing the way in which her head angled slightly to the left as she mused, the curls on that side now brushing against her shoulder. "I suppose that you waited for more evidence this time, and of course, you know your cousins better than you pretended to know Jane."

He flinched a bit at her honest appraisal, but any lingering discomfort attached to his behaviour at Netherfield had been well earned. "Very well, I deserved that."

She smiled ruefully up at him. "I did not mean to be harsh."

"You were only being honest, Miss Bennet. Anything else?"

"You did not pretend to know Anne or the colonel's mind," she said slowly, her chin dipping down. "You warned him, but you did not attempt to persuade him."

"Not that Fitzwilliam would be persuadable even if I had," Darcy remarked, amused.

Miss Elizabeth pressed her lips together and looked off to the side, away from him. "And this time, you were not arguing from self-interest, for it would have been better for you had you encouraged the marriage."

That was the point he had been attempting to make. "Precisely." He gave her a sheepish glance when she shook her head at him.

"If Anne should wed Fitzwilliam," he explained, "I will no longer have to deny the rumours of a betrothal between myself and Anne. Not only that, I shall be able to give up my duty to Rosings, which could not come at a better time as I am hoping to spend more time at Pemberley in the near future." He smiled mischievously. "Fitzwilliam threw me out of the study the other day, and I had no idea what to do. In the end, I was able to spend nearly two hours together in the library with no need for a candle. Quite a novelty, and a rather pleasant one."

"You spent thirty minutes in the library at Netherfield when I was in the room," Miss Elizabeth reminded him slyly. "Though I was unsure you knew I was there. You never said a word."

"That is because I was still fighting my feelings for you," he told her. "You are not the woman a Darcy is supposed to marry, after all."

"And why is that?" she inquired acerbically. "Because I have no money or connections?"

"No," Darcy replied, thrilled she had responded as he predicted. "Because you are headstrong, opinionated, and—" he leaned over so he might lower his voice—"intelligent enough to see me for who I am." He took her hand.

She shook her head and glanced almost shyly at him. "I believed the role you played. That you thought yourself infallible."

He released her hand. "Do you think I do not know I am fallible? I *know*. But I cannot allow others to know, or they will take advantage. Barnaby attempted to take advantage of Fitzwilliam, and he is a *colonel,* for pity's sake."

"Mr. Darcy," Miss Elizabeth said and reached for his hand again. He allowed her to take it. "I do not know who this Barnaby is, and I truly do not care. I said I *believed* that of you. I do not think so *now*. If you recall, I wept because I was angry with myself, not with you. That I could see evidence of your goodness in so many ways and yet immediately think the worst of you again was galling to me. I believed myself wiser."

He lifted her hand to his lips. "I did spend two months showing you that I was precisely the sort of man who would interfere in the lives of others without a care for anything but my own comfort. You cannot be faulted for such a response after only a few weeks."

"I ought to be rational enough to understand that we were both wrong," she murmured. A little line appeared above the bridge of her nose and he longed to smooth it away. He refrained.

"I shall work to improve in this regard."

Miss Elizabeth's sad gaze met his. "I shall, too."

"Miss Bennet, forgive me, but . . . is there aught else?"

Her eyes welled, but the tears did not fall. Thank goodness, for he was not certain he could bear another bout of weeping today.

"I had a letter from my father."

"His response?"

She nodded. "The substance of it was a terrible disappointment. Perhaps I was uncertain of you because of my disappointment in him."

Darcy had been waiting nearly an hour to have this conversation, so he squelched the impulse to interrupt and say that her father was an idiot. Not that she would have taken that well. Safer to simply listen.

"It is only recently that I have seen my own father with the eyes of a woman and not a girl." She smiled wistfully. "He rather favours me, you see, and so I thought him very wise and discerning."

Darcy returned that small smile when she made a joke at her own expense. "As you are aware, I favour you myself, so I cannot fault his choice."

She shook her head. "He loves me, but . . . I have learnt he does not really think well of me, in the end."

"I cannot believe that, Miss Bennet," he murmured, but she only sighed.

"Before Mr. Bingley arrived, my mother was rather excited about our new neighbour." She pulled a face. "I am sure you can imagine the scene. But when I read Papa's letter today, it put me in mind of something he said then, that his daughters were 'silly and ignorant, like other girls,' and distinguished me only by saying that I might have a bit more 'quickness' than the others. It was very like him to say such a thing, and so at the time, I gave it little thought."

"He was probably only teasing, Miss Elizabeth." Darcy had only met the man a few times in Hertfordshire, and he had not cared for the man's sarcastic wit, so different from his daughter's.

She shook her head. "It was as if, after a lifetime of laughing at his jokes, the scales fell from my eyes. He is fond of us all in his own way, but he does not think *really* well of any of us, not even me. It was rather a humbling discovery."

"My apologies, Miss Bennet, but I still do not follow. What did you realise?"

"I love my father, Mr. Darcy. But although he supported me when I refused Mr. Collins's offer—"

"Mr. Collins made you an offer?" Darcy asked, quietly horrified. "Of marriage?"

"Yes," she said, her eyes suddenly alight with mirth, "and more than once, but that is a story for another time, I think."

Proposed? More than once?

With some difficulty, Darcy dragged his attention away from the dark thoughts of Mr. Collins proposing to the woman he meant to make his wife. He might have lost her, and the realisation turned his blood cold. But Miss Elizabeth was still speaking.

"My point is that although I love my father, I no longer truly trust him to protect us."

Darcy forced himself to ask, "And why is that, Miss Bennet?"

"Because he does not take me seriously, Mr. Darcy, particularly not when I am asking him to act on our behalf. I was certain that he did. It was rather a blow to my vanity, for I had always cherished my ability to accurately sketch a person's character. I have been so wrong. First with you, then Mr.

Wickham, your family, and now even with my own father. Perhaps the only people here in Kent I have not judged wrongly are Maria Lucas and Mr. Collins." Her chuckle was forced. "I hardly know myself. I feel . . . rather lost, in fact."

Her expression pinched into something like embarrassment and pain. Darcy could not abide it.

"I read that letter."

"You did, sir."

"It was a good letter. Logical, reasoned. If he did not accept the soundness of the advice, it is not your fault. If you do not mind my asking, what was his response?"

She frowned. "Rather than promising to keep my sisters safe from the man, he teased me about it. He asked how I could believe such a dramatic tale from the daughter of Mr. Collins's beloved patroness and a man I hardly knew. He accused me of jealousy because Mr. Wickham has shifted his affections to another."

Darcy was deeply affronted on Elizabeth's behalf. He had half a mind to call for his horse and ride the fifty miles to Longbourn to have a word with Mr. Bennet. But that would be foolish when he hoped to soon be requesting the man's blessing to wed Miss Elizabeth.

There was a good deal to discuss in her confession, from her previous feelings about him to the attention Wickham had apparently been paying her. But Darcy focused on Miss Elizabeth's most pressing concern. "I assure you that disappointing fathers are not limited to daughters," he said quietly.

Miss Elizabeth nodded at him. "My father was not paying attention if he did not realise that while I enjoyed Mr. Wickham's company at first, I never sought his particular attentions." She rubbed one ear on her shoulder before catching herself. "I thought perhaps that if I was so wrong about my father, whom I have known all my life, then I might be wrong about the feelings I have developed for you."

He shook his head even as his heart leapt to hear that admission. "Your relationship with your father began when you were a child. Now that you are older, it is only natural that you would begin to see the people in your life more clearly. And you were not entirely wrong about me in Hertfordshire. You saw what I wanted you to see." Darcy sighed. "I do play a role, or . . . wear a mask, I suppose. It is not something I relish. In fact, it is exhausting. I fear that before I met you, Miss Bennet, I was *becoming* the man the mask portrayed. And I do not wish to become that man."

"Very good," Miss Elizabeth replied impertinently, "for I should never allow it. That man was thoroughly unpleasant. I much prefer the one standing before me."

He chuckled. "Let the rest of the world say that I married foolishly. You and I shall know the truth. In asking you to be my wife, I shall be making the wisest decision of my life."

Miss Elizabeth turned all the force of her fine eyes upon him. At present, they were sparkling with humour. "I will not argue with that."

"A miracle," he replied drily. "I have at last found a subject upon which we agree."

She laughed a little. "I do not know if it is the most sensible decision you might make," she told him sweetly. "But it will be the one best suited to your happiness. For I intend to make my husband very happy indeed."

"Vexed and confused, you mean."

She smiled widely. "Of course."

"Elizabeth," he said lovingly, and her eyes widened at his use of her Christian name. "I love you, and more than that, I *need* you. If you will have me, I promise that I will never dismiss you or your thoughts. If we disagree, I will never dismiss your concerns out of hand. You will always have my respect. I promise you this."

"You never make a promise unless you know you can fulfil it," she whispered to him.

"Never," he agreed.

Unfortunately, before she could say any more, they were interrupted.

"I disagree," Anne said from where she and Fitzwilliam were approaching. "You said we ought to let the men in and speak with them. I was just so angry with Richard for denying what I was sure he felt."

Darcy silently wished Anne to the devil. Could she not ever keep her own counsel?

"Which was?" Fitzwilliam asked lightly.

Fitzwilliam too. They could go together.

Anne slapped her betrothed in the chest with the back of her hand. "That you have been in love with me as long as I have been in love with you. That you panicked because you thought word would get back to Rosings that Darcy and I had been seen in an amorous embrace."

"Nothing of the sort!" Darcy exclaimed before he could stop himself.

"Well of course not." Anne turned to him with the same incredulous expression she had given Fitzwilliam. "But how would my mother have interpreted the gossip, do you think? My point is that Richard knew that you and I would never marry. *Ever.*"

"That was very emphatic," Miss Elizabeth said softly. Darcy laughed as he pinched the bridge of his nose.

"And yet," Anne continued, eyeing them all warningly, "he acted anyway because he could not bear even the thought of losing me."

"What are you about, woman?" Fitzwilliam asked with some warmth.

"You admitted it yourself, Richard," Anne responded impatiently. "There was no reason at all for you to break Darcy and me apart as you did. And do not claim it was for some noble reason like saving us from a forced marriage. You pushed Darcy away because you love me and did not want him to have me, even if by accident."

"You did gaze into each other's eyes in a way that was very romantic," Miss Elizabeth added teasingly.

"We did," Anne agreed. "Tell everyone that it is so, Richard."

Fitzwilliam glanced uncomfortably at Darcy.

"Confess it," Anne repeated.

"Very well," Fitzwilliam said, and cleared his throat. "I love you. Though at this moment I am not precisely certain why . . ."

"Yes, you are," Anne protested. "You gave me my first kiss, Richard Fitzwilliam, do not you deny it."

Chapter Eleven

Mr. Darcy's mouth fell open, and it was a few seconds before he closed it. "You what? You never said a thing!"

"Are you speaking to me or to Richard, Darcy?" Anne asked impertinently.

"To you both!" Mr. Darcy exclaimed. "When did this happen?"

Fitzwilliam and Anne shared a glance.

"A few hours before Wickham accosted me," Anne said at last. "Apparently he had been watching us and thought if I would kiss Richard, I would kiss him too."

"I tried to tell your father as much," Colonel Fitzwilliam said ruefully, "but Wickham had already told his lies, and Uncle Darcy threw me out."

"But that was years ago. Why have you not offered for Anne before now?"

The colonel shook his head. "We were hardly more than children, Darcy. I returned to training almost immediately, and then was sent abroad. It was years before we saw one another again, and I had no reason to believe Anne still cared for me. She barely looked at me, and I supposed she had entirely forgotten."

"I beg your pardon, Colonel," Elizabeth said, "but no woman forgets her first kiss."

Darcy narrowed his eyes at Miss Elizabeth while Anne nodded smugly.

Fitzwilliam shrugged inelegantly. "I am not a particularly good match. I wanted Anne, not Rosings, but by the time I returned home, my aunt insisted on her marrying Darcy, and I knew it was impossible. So I tucked those feelings away as a youthful infatuation, best forgotten."

"Fool," Anne told him, but she patted his cheek softly. "You were afraid of my mother."

Fitzwilliam offered her a lopsided smile. "That as well. She has never liked me."

"That is not quite true," Mr. Darcy said. "Now that I think on it, she was pleased enough with you before the incident at Pemberley."

Elizabeth thought of everything she had been told about Lady Catherine. Her aloofness, her sense of superiority, but above all, her love for her late husband and the daughter she had accepted as her own. "Anne," she said, thinking aloud, "you never told your mother about what Mr. Wickham had done in importuning you."

"No," Anne agreed.

"Mr. Darcy," Elizabeth said as she turned to face him.

"Yes, Miss Bennet?"

He met her gaze steadily, and whatever Elizabeth was about to say temporarily fled. She blinked before she remembered. "Lady Catherine must have inquired why her other nephew was leaving Pemberley so abruptly."

"I did not think she knew that anything had happened at all, but it is possible."

Elizabeth thought that there was very little Lady Catherine did not notice, particularly in regards to Anne. "If she *did* notice, would she have asked your father for an explanation?" She could not imagine that Lady Catherine would not demand one.

Mr. Darcy nodded. "If she noticed that Fitzwilliam had gone, she would have sought answers. And my father would have said . . ."

Colonel Fitzwilliam looked up at the ceiling. "That I had kissed Anne when she did not want it and struck Wickham to keep him from telling."

Mr. Darcy frowned. "Is that what he said? I never knew, for my father spoke with Wickham alone."

Fitzwilliam nodded. "Uncle Darcy said as much, just before he sent me away."

"You left," Anne said quietly, "and I never knew why. I thought perhaps you did not want me anymore after . . ."

Colonel Fitzwilliam sputtered in shock for a moment before regaining his senses. "Anne, I would *never* have gone, but Uncle Darcy banished me. And then when I finally saw you again, you were so different, I thought . . ."

"*You* try to bear up against Lady Catherine de Bourgh when your heart is broken!" Anne cried out. "The more I withdrew into melancholy, the worse I felt and the harder she tried to protect me. In the end I could hardly stir out of my chambers without being told I was too weak. Between the cosseting and the tonics, I thought I should never recover."

"I suppose that this is the result of keeping secrets," Elizabeth said with a sigh. "It is certainly instructive."

Mr. Darcy scrubbed his face with one hand. Elizabeth had never seen him so unguarded.

"Each of us had part of the story but required the whole of it," he said. "What a mess. Anne was badly shaken by the event. If Fitzwilliam had been allowed to comfort her, all might have been well."

"I began to feel more myself again several years ago, when Mother first made noises about actually planning my marriage to Darcy. But it was not until you came, Elizabeth, and showed me it was possible to say no to my mother, that I truly found my courage again." Anne offered her a wan smile.

It was a very kind thing to say, and Elizabeth demurred. "You acted because it was time, Anne, that is all."

"Past time, rather," Anne replied. "But we are all here now, and finally betrothed!"

"You two are betrothed," Mr. Darcy corrected his cousin. "Miss Bennet and I are courting."

Elizabeth's heart swelled with affection. She had not yet answered him and though she had offered every other indication that she would accept him, Mr. Darcy would not presume.

"Still?" Anne asked, her tone derisive. "What are you waiting for, Darcy?"

He laughed and shook his head. "I am a gentleman, Anne. I am waiting for Miss Bennet to be ready."

She was ready to accept him, but she would not do so until they were alone again. "I must say," Elizabeth informed Anne pertly, "that you are in no position to be chiding anyone about how long it has taken to effect an engagement."

Anne laughed loudly at that. "That is very true! Only I wish we could be married on the same day, Elizabeth."

She shook her head. "I should like to be married from Longbourn, Anne, with my family." Her feelings for Mr. Darcy might have changed, but she would still prefer more time before the wedding so that they had time to know one another even better.

"Oh, of course," Anne replied. "But you will remain in Kent long enough to attend ours?"

"If it is soon and my father permits it, then yes, I should be delighted."

"In the meantime," Mr. Darcy said in that commanding way of his, "Fitzwilliam and Anne might wish to have a rather overdue conversation with Lady Catherine."

"She thought it was *Richard* making me so frightened all this time," Anne said, almost to herself. "No *wonder* she never left us alone when he came with you, Darcy. I ought never to have kept this from her."

"I will not say it, Anne," Mr. Darcy said, "but . . ."

Anne wagged a slender finger at her cousin. "If you say 'I told you so,' I swear, Darcy, I will scratch the leather on your new boots!"

Elizabeth looked up at Mr. Darcy, who was making a valiant effort not to laugh. Having her diminutive friend threatening the very tall, very strong Mr. Darcy *was* a little humorous. "If you do so you shall have to deal with Slipworth, not with me. I would be very careful there, Anne."

"Come, my dear," the colonel said with a light-hearted grin. "Let us enter the lion's den. And Darcy," he said over his shoulder, "just for being smug, you must now join us. Bring Miss Bennet along with you."

Elizabeth shook her head in short, rapid bursts, but Mr. Darcy only laughed at her. Laughed!

"Oh, no, Miss Bennet," he said, tucking her hand into the crook of his arm. "I am not facing my aunt without you."

"Oh, wait!" Anne said. "I cannot go just yet. Darcy, Fitzwilliam—out."

Darcy blew out another breath and rubbed the back of his neck. He wished there was a chair nearby, but he had been strictly instructed to wait here with Fitzwilliam. He had never loitered so long in a hallway in his life. "How long is this meant to take?"

"Will you stop complaining?" Fitzwilliam snapped. "How am I to know how long a lady requires to complete her toilette?"

"You are both very impatient," Miss Elizabeth said as she emerged from Anne's sitting room to join them. "Women often take days to plan a single ensemble for a ball. Anne was very efficient."

Not a minute later, Anne swept out of the room. Her hair was pinned up in a becoming style with two golden curls framing her face. She was wearing a gown Darcy had never seen before, one that not only fit her properly, but accentuated her tiny waist and complemented her petite figure. It was only a morning gown, white with corded short sleeves that were decorated with two small tassels each, but it was both elegant and womanly, and Fitzwilliam swallowed audibly when he saw her.

"She was worth waiting for, Colonel, would not you say?" Miss Elizabeth asked pertly.

"Always," Fitzwilliam concurred, without taking his eyes off his intended. He offered Anne a little bow and his arm.

"Thank goodness Mrs. Abernathy completed this one so quickly. I am ready to face Mother now."

Elizabeth offered her an encouraging smile.

"Come," Anne said, her voice not as strong as normal.

Darcy and Miss Elizabeth fell in behind the couple. "You will not allow Lady Catherine to send me off to the colonies, Mr. Darcy?"

"Not unless I am sent with you," he replied easily.

Elizabeth blushed. "As to that," she said softly, glancing at the other couple as they descended the stairs, "I should offer you an answer to the question you posed earlier."

His expression grew sombre, and he stopped to look at her. "You need not. I am willing to wait if you require time."

She shook her head. "I do not need to wait."

"Very well."

It was best to be quick about it lest they be interrupted yet again. "My answer is yes, Mr. Darcy."

"Yes," he whispered, such a warm expression of delight stealing across his features that Elizabeth could not help but smile. "Do you promise?"

She reached up to touch the palm of her hand to his cheek. He placed his own hand over hers. "I give you my word."

Mr. Darcy took both of her hands in his. "When?"

"Late summer at the earliest, sir," she warned him teasingly.

"So long?" he inquired, for all the world like a small child being sent upstairs before dinner.

It could not fail to amuse Elizabeth. "Did you not just say you would wait until I was ready?"

"That," he said, gazing into her eyes with a heat that made her heart beat harder, "was *before* you said yes."

She shook her head at him. "After your cousins marry and I return to Longbourn, you may approach my father. And once he is won over, we must allow my mother her time to exhibit."

He chuckled. "That is fair, I suppose. I would not deny her."

Her response was arch. "You may not be entirely hopeless after all, Mr. Darcy."

"No," he agreed cheerfully, "for I did not even point out that when we spoke about marriage earlier, I did not actually pose a question at all. I only made a statement."

"I rescind my compliment," Elizabeth replied pertly. "You are *entirely* hopeless."

Darcy was very nearly giddy with happiness. He offered her his arm, and Elizabeth, *his Elizabeth*, took it as they turned together towards the stairs.

After glancing up at him and offering an almost shy smile, she took a little breath and took up their previous subject. "Anne is anxious."

Darcy pushed his elation away with a practised hand. They would help his cousins and then return to their own joy, though it remained humming somewhere deep inside him. "I surmised as much. She has never been able to stand up to her mother."

"Why is that?"

Mr. Darcy smiled. "You have met Lady Catherine."

"True. But Lady Catherine is Anne's mother in every way that matters. They truly love one another."

"Which is why it is so difficult for Anne to displease her."

Miss Elizabeth sighed. "It grieves me that a mother's love would create such anxiety, but I have some experience in this area."

"Anne has come into her own these past weeks, with you as her friend. But she was of a more retiring nature than her mother even before the incident at Pemberley."

The Anne Elizabeth knew was not retiring, but she would not argue the fact. "Is there anyone in England who is *not* of a more retiring nature than your aunt?"

"Lady Catherine's brother the earl, when he is giving a speech in the House of Lords." Darcy smiled at her. "Otherwise, no."

All teasing came to a stop when Anne hesitated just outside her mother's sitting room. She took a deep breath.

"I am here with you, Anne," Fitzwilliam said. "You need not face her alone."

Anne shot him a sly look. "She expects bad news from you. But she *loves* me."

Fitzwilliam laughed. "Very well, perhaps I am not the best partner for this particular conference, but I am afraid I must insist. We shall all be friends before long, you will see."

Chapter Twelve

Darcy and Miss Elizabeth shared another look before they followed his cousins into the drawing room. The colour that rose to her cheeks was enchanting, and he struggled to focus on the matter at hand.

His aunt was sitting in another of her chairs that resembled a throne. She had one in nearly every public room.

"Anne, what *are* you wearing?" From the twisted set of her lips, it was obvious that Lady Catherine did not approve of her daughter's new fashions.

"I am wearing one of Mrs. Abernathy's wonderful gowns," Anne said weakly, and turned to show off the sleeves. "Miss Bennet helped me select it."

Elizabeth glared at Anne, who shrank back.

"Miss Bennet?" Lady Catherine rose to her feet and pointed regally at Miss Elizabeth. "You will leave this house at once. We need none of your influence on Miss de Bourgh here."

"No, Mother," Anne said faintly. "Miss Bennet is my friend."

Lady Catherine was unimpressed. She pointed the end of her cane at Miss Elizabeth. "Miss *Bennet* is the sort of woman you like for a friend?

One of a half-dozen unwed girls who belong to an entailed estate? Why would you select such a girl as your friend? You are so much higher than she."

"Five daughters," Darcy corrected his aunt, ignoring the jab in his ribs from Miss Elizabeth's sharp elbow. "There are only five." Soon there would be only four.

Fortunately, all his aunt had time to do was cast a dismissive look at him before Anne drew her attention again.

"To be honest, Mother," Anne said, "at first I liked Miss Bennet for the way she stood up to you."

Darcy heard a soft groan from Miss Elizabeth.

"It will be well," he whispered.

"For *you*," she whispered back. "Everything Anne says sinks me further in your aunt's esteem. Not that I stood very high to begin with."

Her mother's stare was icy. "You would have me believe that Miss Bennet—that headstrong girl there—was in any danger of being cowed? Absurd."

"No, but neither would I have you believe that denigrating her relations was all that is proper."

"I did no such thing!"

Anne looked over her shoulder at them, sending a contrite glance in Miss Elizabeth's direction before replying. "You do not recall saying that her sisters ought not be out at the same time? That they ought to have had a governess? You were publicly criticizing her parents."

Darcy stole a glance at Fitzwilliam, who was watching the confrontation with the shadow of a smile.

"There is nothing denigrating in speaking the truth," Lady Catherine declared.

"What about offering her a place in my companion's room to practice her music?" Anne was persistent. "You must be aware that she is a gentleman's daughter and not a servant. And you might at least have asked Mrs. Jenkinson if she was willing to share her room before you offered it up. Those are her private chambers."

"All the rooms belong to Rosings. Mrs. Jenkinson does not own the room."

"Neither do you."

Darcy sucked in a breath. Lady Catherine had a generous jointure and lifetime rights to live at Rosings, but the estate itself was held in a trust for Anne.

"Anne," Fitzwilliam said, his voice firm and low, "it is enough."

Anne pressed her lips together and stopped speaking.

Lady Catherine composed herself. "Anne, why would you not seek me out if you wished to purchase new clothes?"

"*Anne*," Miss Elizabeth hissed. "You promised you would tell Lady Catherine I suggested that very thing."

Anne did not look up. "I could not do it, Elizabeth. I am sorry."

Miss Elizabeth frowned. "Friends keep their promises, Anne," she said firmly, still whispering, "or they do not make them."

"Forgive me?" Anne whispered back.

She was answered with a nod, but Darcy was sure they would speak more later. He was beginning to understand Elizabeth very well.

"Elizabeth?" his aunt cried, and for a moment he thought he had spoken aloud. But Lady Catherine was only responding to Anne. "*Elizabeth*? I see it now. You have turned my daughter against me! *Everything* changed when you came to Rosings. Darcy has turned away from Anne, and Richard Fitzwilliam was there to take the prize." She glared at Fitzwilliam. "I know it all!"

"You are wrong." Anne was still gazing on the floor. What could be so interesting there, Darcy did not know.

"Anne, you must show your mother that you are strong enough to make these choices," he told her.

"And you cannot do that," Fitzwilliam added gently, "with your eyes upon the ground. I need you to stand up for me, love. For me, for Darcy, for Miss Bennet, and most of all, for yourself. Can you do that?"

Anne swallowed, took a very deep breath, and slowly, slowly raised her chin until she met her mother's eye. She took half a step forward and said, more steadily, "Mother, Miss Bennet insisted I inform you about the dresses. I promised I would, but I did not do it. I tried, but you are always so . . . sure of your own opinions. I did not wish to upset you."

"You ought to have informed me regardless."

"Yes. But you would have made a fuss, and I wanted new dresses. Dresses like this one."

Lady Catherine eyed her daughter and nearly smiled at Anne standing up to her. "I see." Her gimlet eye fell on Miss Elizabeth next. "Very well, I am glad to hear that Miss Bennet has sense enough to know what is due to me as your mother." She held up one bejewelled hand as though she was offering a royal pardon. "She may stay."

"That is not the worst of it," Anne said.

Lady Catherine looked at Anne askance.

Anne faltered.

"Go ahead, Anne," Miss Elizabeth said gently. "Your mother deserves to hear this too."

"When we visited Pemberley the summer I was sixteen . . ." Anne stumbled over the words.

"You need not speak of it," Lady Catherine announced. "I am aware. I have always been aware."

"You only think that because I was afraid to tell you. Richard kissed me, yes, but I wanted him to. I love him, Mother. I loved him then, and I still do. It was George Wickham who accosted me a few hours later."

"The steward's son?"

For a moment, Darcy was put in mind of a Leviathan rising from the deep. Lady Catherine seemed to grow several feet taller as she stood, snarling his name. "George Wickham?"

"Yes. He threatened to tell everyone that I had done more than kiss Richard unless I kissed him too. I said no, but he would not allow me to leave."

"Anne," Miss Elizabeth murmured. "Tell her the rest."

There was more? Both Darcy and Fitzwilliam turned to Anne.

His tiny cousin balled her fists tightly and raised her chin. "He attempted to abscond with me."

His aunt's complexion paled, and her breath seemed to catch in her chest. He and Fitzwilliam stepped forward together, but she waved them off. "Anne, he did not . . ."

"No, Mother, he did not, because Richard arrived to save me."

"Had I known it all," Richard said darkly, "he would not have left those woods."

"Then it is a good thing I did not tell you," Anne told him quietly. "For a man like George Wickham is not worth your life."

For perhaps the very first time in Darcy's memory, Lady Catherine was flustered. She began to speak, then stopped. Finally, she asked, "Why did Darcy's father tell me it was Richard's doing?"

Anne pulled a face. "Because Mr. Wickham lied, and Uncle Darcy believed him."

Lady Catherine was still baffled. "George Darcy believed the steward's son over the son of an earl—his own nephew? Why would a Fitzwilliam be jealous of someone like George Wickham?"

Darcy shook his head. "I cannot say, Aunt. His father was a great friend to mine, and I have met many stewards and their sons who are honourable men. Alas, George Wickham is not among them, and my father would never see it."

Aunt Catherine held out her hand to Anne, who nearly sobbed as she took it. "You were so changed by that visit," she said, more gently than Darcy had ever heard her speak. She touched Anne's cheek tenderly. "You slept the day away, you picked at your food. I did not know what was wrong, so I wrote to your Uncle Darcy and demanded to know what had happened. You always defended Richard, but he ran off without a word, and I thought he must be responsible somehow."

Fitzwilliam stepped forward. "I was sent off, Aunt Catherine. I apologise. We should have told you."

"Yes," she said harshly. "*Someone* should have."

"I was afraid you would do something out of anger, something dangerous, and put yourself at risk," Anne said earnestly. "You would have, too."

Lady Catherine pulled Anne into an embrace, but she did not deny it.

"My goodness, Eliza!" Charlotte said after Elizabeth had finished the tale. "Only think, Miss de Bourgh was not ill at all, only pining for Colonel Fitzwilliam!"

That was not all it had been, of course, but Elizabeth did not dispute it.

"It is so romantic," Maria crowed. "Imagine, Mr. Wickham a villain! Oh, I cannot wait to tell the story to everyone at home!" She nearly danced up the stairs, where Elizabeth presumed she would write several letters to be sent to Meryton post-haste.

Elizabeth hoped Maria's letters would do the job Papa had refused to accept.

"Will you stay longer in Kent, Eliza?" Charlotte inquired. "Although no date has been set for the wedding, I am certain you will be invited to the wedding breakfast."

"Anne has already requested that I attend her," Elizabeth informed Charlotte.

"Oh, my dear," Charlotte said, deeply pleased. "You have become a very useful friend for Miss de Bourgh."

"I suppose I have, though I could not have foreseen it."

"Of course not," Charlotte said, "but will this friendship not bring you into Mr. Darcy's circle? I am sure he only wants the opportunity to make you an offer."

"He does not want for an opportunity," Elizabeth said, then waited.

"What do you mean?" Charlotte gasped. "He has already asked! Eliza, how sly you have been!"

Elizabeth smiled. "I await only the date of Anne's wedding and then will write for permission to extend my stay until then if you will have me. Will Maria be willing to remain? I fear my uncle cannot spare his manservant twice."

"I do not think we could tear her away," Charlotte said wryly. "She will have filled an entire journal with all the goings on. Lucas Lodge will be a very dull place in comparison. And yes, of course we shall have you for as long as you care to remain." She lifted her brows. "Though I daresay Mr. Darcy would be only too happy to escort you back himself."

Elizabeth smiled.

"Dare I ask more about your understanding?"

"Mr. Darcy will write to my father. Once we leave Kent, we will travel to London as planned. Jane and I will return to Longbourn from there, and Mr. Darcy believes he will be allowed to stay at Netherfield until we are wed."

"I am so happy for you, dearest."

"Thank you. It does not feel entirely real. When I arrived in Kent, I had no idea what the outcome of my stay would be."

"Of course not. You and Mr. Darcy were required to step back and clear away many misunderstandings before you could truly begin again."

"Will you think less of me if I admit that once we had done so, I moved from dislike to admiration and respect without delay? And that love was not far behind?"

Charlotte smiled. "I suspected it might be the case. And I am very happy for you."

Elizabeth smiled. "It may be immodest, but I will say that I am also pleased for myself. Not the least in imagining what Mr. Bingley's sisters will suffer when they hear of Mr. Darcy's choice of bride."

They were still laughing when Mr. Collins entered the house. He frowned at them both and hurried away to his study.

Her father's letter, an unprecedented second missive from him in the short span of a month, offered his permission for her to remain, but was otherwise full of quips that Elizabeth no longer found amusing. It was his way, she supposed, of offering her his tentative approval.

"Do be sure to make your way back to Longbourn before you marry, Lizzy," he had written in the end, perhaps the only serious statement he had penned. "You may be destined to become Mrs. Darcy, but you will remain Elizabeth Bennet until we have spoken together. I will not have you regret your choice of partner in life."

Elizabeth folded the paper and placed the letter back in her pocket. She gazed out over the field of tulips, some which were beginning to turn brown around the edges and droop.

It was a great deal of effort for such a transitory effect, but Elizabeth could not complain. There was something deeply soothing about being here.

She held two letters that she had already read through once. The one from her Aunt Gardiner had been all that was cheerful and congratulatory, though she did confess to some surprise. That was better than the one from Jane, who had simply proclaimed herself "amazed" and begged Elizabeth not to marry unless she felt what she ought for her betrothed. The similarities between her dearest sister and her dearest Mr. Darcy had never been so clear.

After having taken such a vocal dislike to Mr. Darcy last autumn, Elizabeth knew she deserved her sister's disbelief. And she would not be the only one. Jane's letter hinted that Mr. Bingley was also anxious to hear their tale. It seemed that he had become a frequent visitor at Gracechurch Street. Elizabeth wondered if she might not be a part of a double wedding after all.

Mr. Darcy and the colonel had departed for a few days to tend to business in London, but they had returned exactly when they said that they would, and Colonel Fitzwilliam would wed Anne tomorrow. The day after, the newly married couple would travel to Brighton. Elizabeth and Maria would return to London in Mr. Darcy's carriage, with him riding alongside, and Maria could barely speak for all her excitement at the prospect.

Elizabeth had meant to be in Kent for six weeks. It had been nearly ten now, and she and Mr. Darcy continued to court under the watchful eyes of an inordinately pleased Charlotte and a haughty but accepting Lady Catherine, as they could not announce an engagement until they received her father's formal approval.

"Good day, Miss Elizabeth."

Elizabeth folded her letters and tucked them away before she looked up with a smile. He had reverted to calling her Miss Elizabeth even though Jane was not here. "Good day, Mr. Darcy."

He was so very handsome, her intended. His dark curls were tousled by the light breeze, and he stood above her straight and tall.

Very tall.

He was wearing the green coat he knew was a favourite of hers, and his breeches fit him perfectly in all the best ways. She might have been embarrassed to notice, once, but now that she was to wed—for she would not accept any other outcome—she felt she was not only allowed but obliged to observe how very attractive her Mr. Darcy was.

"I am always able to find you here," he said agreeably, and held out a hand to her. She took it, and he helped her to her feet.

"It is no proof of intelligence on your part, then," Elizabeth replied lightly.

He shook his head at her. "Are you ready to return to the parsonage, or do we have time to visit your grove? For tomorrow will be the wedding and the breakfast, and the day after we shall depart quite early. It will be your last chance to see it. On this trip, at least."

"Mr. Darcy," she replied as she slipped her hand under his proffered arm, "you need not provide me with ready excuses. If you are asking whether I should like to spend more time with you, the answer is yes."

"Yes is the word I most like to hear you say to me," he told her.

"How fortunate," Elizabeth told him, reaching up to straighten his coat, though there was not a single wrinkle. "For I plan to say it as often as I can."

Epilogue

Darcy and Fitzwilliam were sitting at a corner table in their London club when a familiar, undesirable voice wafted over the air to them.

"You must congratulate me, gentlemen!"

Darcy glanced up, noting that the man's clothes were finer than any he had worn in some time.

"Why is that?" Fitzwilliam inquired.

"I am wed to the Baroness of Wilhemsberg!"

Darcy cleared his throat and shot a look at his cousin before responding. "Congratulations, Wickham."

Fitzwilliam snickered behind a closed fist. "Congratulations," he said, though it was muffled.

"Come, gentlemen," Wickham continued, smiling broadly. "This is a fine way to behave. You must buy me a drink."

"I shall not," Darcy said quietly. "You have had enough money from my family, Wickham, and have now made a very eligible match with a German baroness. You can have no need of anything further from me, or the master of Rosings, here." He nodded at Fitzwilliam.

Fitzwilliam and Anne had been wed more than seven months now. He himself had been wed for nearly four.

Four glorious months. Upon receiving Mr. Bennet's surprised consent to wed Elizabeth, Darcy had returned to Netherfield to woo her in earnest. He had been in residence even before Bingley arrived in Hertfordshire to continue his own courtship of Elizabeth's eldest sister. During the warm, sunny days of the summer, Darcy and Elizabeth had spoken a great deal about the propensities to judge quickly on Elizabeth's part and to hold tightly to both opinions and grudges on his. Those months, he believed, had made it possible for the two of them to enter their marriage with enthusiasm, for by that time, they knew one another very well.

Wickham appeared a bit uncomfortable being put off by Darcy, but when several other members invited him to the card room, he grinned and offered them a salute as he wandered off.

"Will his luck hold, do you think?" Fitzwilliam asked as he lifted his brandy and took a sip.

"Almost certainly," Darcy responded. "For a time."

"Excellent," Fitzwilliam said. "Excellent."

Darcy consulted his watch precisely twice over the next two hours before placing it back in his pocket and rising from his chair. "I should like to return to Elizabeth," he announced to his cousin. "Shall we see how Wickham fares?"

"Well, he has not been tossed out yet, so I suppose we should," Fitzwilliam replied. "Perhaps there is something we might do to hurry this along."

When they entered the room, they saw that the men were playing commerce, and that for once, Wickham had in fact been lucky. He was down, but not too much.

"Enough of this," grumbled the sallow young man with a mop of sandy brown hair. He tossed down a stack of bank notes.

Wickham pressed his lips together. "That is playing rather high," he said calmly.

"I see we have arrived at just the right moment," Fitzwilliam said in Darcy's ear.

"A Darcy is never late," he replied with a grin.

"No matter, gentlemen," Fitzwilliam said jovially. "Wickham has no doubt told you of his advantageous marriage. I am certain he is able to meet your wager."

"Of course," Wickham said, and added nearly all he had won into the pool.

The men finished the round and the sallow young man laid out his cards. "Four of a kind."

The others groaned, but no one stood from the table. They tossed their money for a new round in the middle of the table.

Wickham appeared stricken.

The winner looked at Wickham. "Are you in?"

"Of course," Wickham replied, tossing in what he had left. "You must allow me the chance to regain my winnings. I shall just write a vowel for the rest."

"None of your vowels here, man," said the man to Wickham's left. "I do not know you."

Wickham was genuinely affronted. "I am married to the baroness . . ."

"Yes, I know. Plenty of titled *English* women with no money floating about London," the man replied and yanked at his ear. "I have no use for the German ones."

As no one moved to contradict that statement, Wickham reached to retrieve his money and withdraw.

"What do you think you are doing?" the man to his right said with a scowl and pushed him away. "You put your blunt in same as the rest. Once the money is in, you cannot retrieve it unless you win the hand."

"Never fear, gentlemen," Fitzwilliam said, "He will be back next quarter. When the baroness gives him his allowance."

The men gathered around the table laughed.

"Wait a minute," the dealer said, leaning over to snap his fingers in Wickham's face. "The baroness . . . I know that woman!" He laughed uproariously, slapping a palm against the table to the complaints of the others. "You have wed the Wily Widow of Wilhemsberg! Good God, man, she must be sixty years old."

"No, that is incorrect," Wickham said glibly, though Darcy thought his complexion a little wan. "You must be thinking of someone else."

"How many German baronesses can there be in London? No, it is she. Has she taken off her wig for you yet?"

The laughter increased.

"I hope you did not wed because you expected to inherit, Wickham," Fitzwilliam said, shaking his head sadly, "for her money belongs to her son, you know." He hauled Wickham up by his arm, freeing up the seat at the table.

"Come, Wickham," he said roughly. "I wish to have a word."

The men who filled the room were still laughing, but soon they were more engaged in their game than the scene that had just played out before them.

Wickham smiled as they walked, charming as ever. "You must have the wrong woman. I am to be my wife's heir, and at her age, it cannot be long."

"My grandmother was nearing eighty when she died," Darcy mused.

"My grandmother is seventy-eight," Fitzwilliam added. "And still alive."

"You do not mean to make yourself a widower through foul means, do you, Wickham?" Darcy inquired, as coolly as he might ask whether the man had tickets to the theatre.

"Of course not," Wickham replied smoothly.

"I am glad to hear it," Darcy said. "For I have it on very good authority that you would be unlikely to survive the attempt. You have met her son, I presume?" Whether Wickham was prevaricating was neither here nor there. He would never succeed, for the baroness was a clever woman, and her son and heir a well-respected patron of Gentleman Jack's.

"I have not had that pleasure."

Darcy and Fitzwilliam chuckled. "He is taller than I am and broader than Fitzwilliam here. And I daresay none too pleased with his mother's *latest* husband."

Wickham's gaze shot to Darcy's.

"Wickham," Darcy said with a sigh. "Did you not even inquire into her past? Do you truly believe your charm was the reason she acquiesced? No other man will have her. She is a widow four times over."

Fitzwilliam slapped Wickham on the back hard enough that the man had to take a quick step forward. "Never you mind. We are almost certain that none of them died by violence. Still," he said thoughtfully, "I should tell my mother that the Baroness has married again. She will find that bit of gossip highly amusing. Your marriage will be the subject of many a visit tomorrow, I dare say."

"Your mother may wish to hurry," Darcy pointed out helpfully. "The gossip will go home with these men, and she does so like to the first to disseminate any news."

Wickham's countenance paled.

"Poor Wickham," Fitzwilliam said, but there was no hint of sympathy in his voice. "Married to a baroness, yet no more the independent gentleman of means you were when you remained unwed."

"Less," Darcy added.

"Come," Fitzwilliam said. "Time for the groom to go home."

"Where did you even meet her?" Darcy asked as they escorted Wickham out. He knew, of course, but he wanted Wickham to put it all together, and the man had not yet done so. Had Wickham always been this dim? Of course he had—that was why it had been so easy to hoist him on his own petard.

After a few seconds ticked away, Wickham's mouth fell open, and he dug his heels into the carpet. "Your aunt was in Brighton when he"—he stabbed a finger at Fitzwilliam—"was on his wedding trip."

Fitzwilliam nodded. "Six weeks in, she did travel to join us. She is my mother now, after all."

"*She* introduced me to the baroness," Wickham said, seething. "You tricked me!"

"Did not you believe you were tricking us?" Darcy asked blandly.

Fitzwilliam frowned. "All I did was suggest to my aunt that you be introduced to the baroness. Anything beyond that was all at your instigation, Wickham."

"You *knew* she had a son. You *knew* her money was an annuity from him."

"I did. He does take excellent care of her. I am not certain how she persuaded him that she should marry you."

"We did not tell him," Wickham muttered.

"I shall greatly anticipate the story of that first meeting, then." Darcy could not help but smile at the thought.

Fitzwilliam barked out a laugh. "Cheer up, Wickham. At least there was no need to take your wife to Gretna, for she is beyond the age of consent."

"Well beyond," Darcy added. "I confess it is something of a mystery to me. Do not you generally prefer younger girls, Wickham?"

"Young girls, Darcy," Fitzwilliam replied, his lips curling down into a severe frown. "Not younger. Young."

Wickham's expression darkened.

"Did you think you would never experience retribution?" Darcy inquired pleasantly. "We did wait a bit to throw you off the scent, as it were, but in the end it was not difficult."

"No, in fact it was quite delightful to watch the Wily Widow seduce you, I must say. But I cannot take all the credit." Fitzwilliam gave Darcy a little bow. "It was Darcy's idea to have my aunt invite her and let nature take its course."

The muscle along Wickham's jaw ticked.

Darcy nodded. "As for your future domicile . . . The baroness may have met you in Brighton, but I hear she prefers Bath, which is a safer location than London for a man in your predicament."

"Bath has not been fashionable in years," Wickham snarled.

Darcy smiled dangerously. "And London is no longer safe. Not for you."

"Do not cross me, Darcy. I have a story that everyone here would absolutely adore."

"They might, but when I tell them that you have married the baroness, I doubt very much that they will believe anything you say. A man so stupid or desperate as to marry her to seek advancement cannot be trusted."

"Besides, you owe the both of us a great deal of money," Fitzwilliam mused.

"I owe you nothing."

"Oh, but you do." Darcy was enjoying this little drama immensely. "We have been rather busy sending men about the country to purchase your most recent debts. You have been quite profligate for a man with such limited resources."

"Go to Bath," Fitzwilliam said. "Live with your wife. Do not return to London, Derbyshire, or Hertfordshire ever again."

"You would never touch me," Wickham said with a nonchalant shrug. "Darcy, at least, is too much the gentleman."

Darcy chuckled darkly. "You think too well of me. No matter, I need not dirty my hands with the likes of you. Your debts to the merchants have been paid, but not your debts of honour. I assure you there are men in all three locations that would like very much to meet with you again."

"London, Derbyshire, and Hertfordshire," Wickham repeated with a glint in his eye. He turned to Fitzwilliam. "What about Kent?"

"Oh, by all means," Fitzwilliam said, his voice as cold as steel. "Come to Kent."

Fitzwilliam grasped one of Wickham's arms and Darcy grabbed the other. Together, they nearly carried him outside.

"I think I need another drink," Fitzwilliam said, dusting his hands off as they watched Wickham pull himself away and stride off, calling for his horse.

"I am for home," Darcy replied, once Wickham was out of sight.

Fitzwilliam threw his head back and laughed. "New-married couples," he teased. "You are hopeless."

Darcy smiled a small, secret smile. Hope*ful*, rather. And happy. Very, very happy.

Elizabeth sighed when he had finished the tale. "After all the pain Mr. Wickham has caused your family, it does not seem enough, somehow."

Darcy shrugged over his soup. "Unfortunately, we could never prove he meant to abscond with Anne so many years ago, and I fortunately prevented his elopement with Georgiana. In the end, my father is the one who perpetuated the worst of it because he refused to act." He reached across the small table to brush her cheek lightly with the back of one hand. "But this marriage will be a lifetime of slow torture for a man like him, Elizabeth. Instead of the important gentleman of means he intended to become, he has voluntarily become the baroness's lapdog."

"That *was* rather clever on your part, dearest," she said sweetly, leaning into his touch. "Do you think he will remain in Bath?"

Darcy gazed down at Elizabeth lovingly and her cheeks flushed a charming shade of pink. "I do not believe the baroness will allow him to leave her," he said reassuringly. "And in Bath he may be important even on his limited funds. He will remain."

"Are we merely foisting him onto other unsuspecting women, though?"

His Elizabeth was always thinking about those who might be vulnerable. He had learned, in their time of courtship, that she and her elder sister were alike in many ways. He chuckled. "I do not think you understand. We chose to introduce Wickham to the baroness precisely because she has a reputation for strictness. She will not allow him to take up with other women or abuse her staff, and her son will use her allowance to ensure Wickham's compliance." He placed their bowls on the tray and made up a plate of food for her. "Wickham is like Aesop's boy with the filberts, but he will never give up what he has grasped, and therefore will never be able to withdraw his hand from the bottle." He set their plates down. "No, it is enough."

"And he will not inherit?" Elizabeth began to eat.

"No. The baroness has only the one son, but there are five grandchildren upon whom she dotes. Wickham had better save his pennies, for anything the baroness does possess will be left to them." He chuckled. "Presuming he survives his first encounter with her son."

Elizabeth's eyes widened, and he hastened to reassure her. "He will not kill Wickham. He will, however, leave no doubt as to who is in charge."

They ate in silence for a time.

"Well then," Elizabeth said as she finished her food and placed her napkin on the table. "I think that is quite enough discussion of Mr. Wickham, sir."

Darcy was only too pleased to comply. "So formal, Elizabeth. Am I not Fitzwilliam to you?"

She tapped her lips with one slender finger. "I have been thinking."

"Always a perilous time for me."

Elizabeth wagged a finger at him. "You call your cousin Fitzwilliam. I shall have to come up with something else for you." She rose to place a kiss on his nose. "Willy?"

His jaw dropped. "You would not dare."

Her eyes lifted to the ceiling. "Wills?"

"That is a child's name," he protested.

She smiled and arched one brow. "William?"

He frowned. "That is so . . . common."

"And you are a man who will always need to learn a little humility, I think. William it is."

Darcy groaned. "Truly?"

Elizabeth laughed. "Perhaps only when I am vexed with you. I shall simply have to begin calling your cousin Richard, as he has said I ought."

"Did he, now?"

"He pointed out how confusing the names are, and I quite agree. We shall not be following this ridiculous tradition of using surnames for first names when we have a son."

Darcy truly did not mind, but he rather *enjoyed* vexing his wife. "It is what Darcys have always done."

She huffed at him. "Not anymore."

"There is one flaw in your reasoning, Elizabeth."

"And what is that, *William*?"

Perfect. "We do not yet have a son."

Her dark eyes narrowed. "And you mean to remedy that, do you?" She saw through him.

He *loved* that she saw through him.

"Very well, Mr. Darcy."

Elizabeth stood and walked to the door that led to their chamber. As she disappeared over the threshold, her silk dressing gown dropped to the floor and his mouth grew as dry as dust.

"Now?" he croaked.

"Yes, Mr. Darcy," she called back to him. "Yes."

The End

Want to read more? Click here for An Accidental Proposal's bonus epilogue

https://BookHip.com/SBJFAZ

Missed one of the Accidental Love books? Click here for the series

https://mybook.to/AccidentalLovePandP

Acknowledgments

Thank you to . . .

My beta, cold, and ARC readers, those who pointed out errors or inconsistencies or just asked the right questions.

My critique partner extraordinaire, Sarah Courtney, who is always ready for an 11pm brainstorm session.

Sarah Pesce of Lopt&Cropt editing, who just makes the book better. Every time.

And of course, thank you to my readers—without you, there would *be* no books. Well, certainly not as many!

About The Author

 Melanie Rachel first read Jane Austen's novels as a girl at summer camp and will always associate them with starry skies and reading by flashlight. She was born and raised in Southern California but has also lived in Pennsylvania, New Jersey, and Washington. She currently makes her home in Arizona where she resides with her husband and their incredibly bossy Jack Russell Terrier.

Want updates on special giveaways and new books? Sign up for Melanie's newsletter at https://www.melanierachelauth or.com/newsletterand all her bonus content at https://www .melanierachelauthor.com/bonus-content. You can also find Melanie at www.melanierachelauthor.com or on Facebook and Instagram at *melanierachelbooks*.

Other Books by the Author

Mr. Darcy's Christmas Letters

An Accidental Scandal

An Accidental Holiday

Interwoven

An Unexpected Inheritance

A Gentleman's Honor

Transforming Mr. Darcy

I Never Knew Myself

Drawing Mr. Darcy (duology)

Headstrong (trilogy)

Courage Requires

Courage Rises

Printed in Great Britain
by Amazon

40626679R00091